North Riverside Public Library District
2400 S. Des Plaines Avenue
North Riverside, IL 60546
708-447-0869
www.northriversidelibrary.org

POWER CODERS

A PECULIAR SEQUENCE OF EVENTS

AMANDA VINK

ILLUSTRATED BY JOEL GENNARI

PowerKiDS press™
New York

Published in 2019 by The Rosen Publishing Group, Inc.
29 East 21st Street, New York, NY 10010

First Edition

Illustrator: Joel Grennari
Interior Layout: Tanya Dellaccio
Managing Editor: Nathalie Beullens-Maoui
Editorial Director: Greg Roza

Library of Congress Cataloging-in-Publication Data

Names: Vink, Amanda, author.
Title: A peculiar sequence of events / Amanda Vink.
Description: New York : PowerKids Press, [2019] | Series: Power Coders | Includes index.
Identifiers: LCCN 2017057848| ISBN 9781538340295 (library bound) | ISBN 9781538340301 (pbk.) | ISBN 9781538340318 (6 pack)
Subjects: | CYAC: Computer programming–Fiction. | Time–Fiction. | Bullying–Fiction.
Classification: LCC PZ7.1.V58 Pec 2019 | DDC [Fic]–dc23
LC record available at https://lccn.loc.gov/2017057848

Manufactured in the United States of America

CPSIA Compliance Information: Batch CS18PK: For Further Information contact Rosen Publishing, New York, New York at 1-800-237-9932

CONTENTS

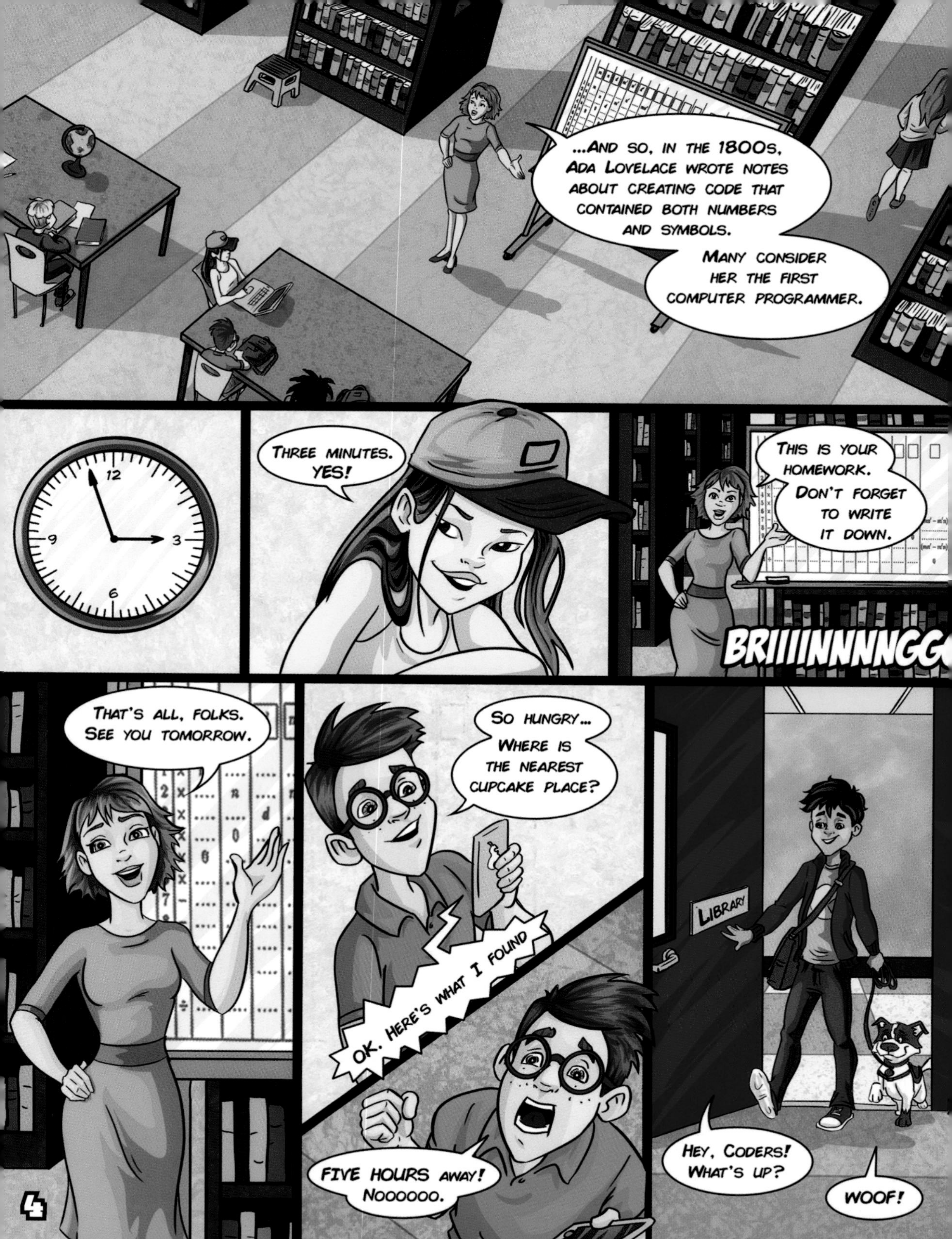

...AND SO, IN THE 1800S, ADA LOVELACE WROTE NOTES ABOUT CREATING CODE THAT CONTAINED BOTH NUMBERS AND SYMBOLS.
MANY CONSIDER HER THE FIRST COMPUTER PROGRAMMER.
THREE MINUTES. YES!
THIS IS YOUR HOMEWORK.
DON'T FORGET TO WRITE IT DOWN.
BRIIIINNNNGG
THAT'S ALL, FOLKS. SEE YOU TOMORROW.
SO HUNGRY... WHERE IS THE NEAREST CUPCAKE PLACE?
OK. HERE'S WHAT I FOUND
FIVE HOURS AWAY! NOOOOOO.
LIBRARY
HEY, CODERS! WHAT'S UP?
WOOF!

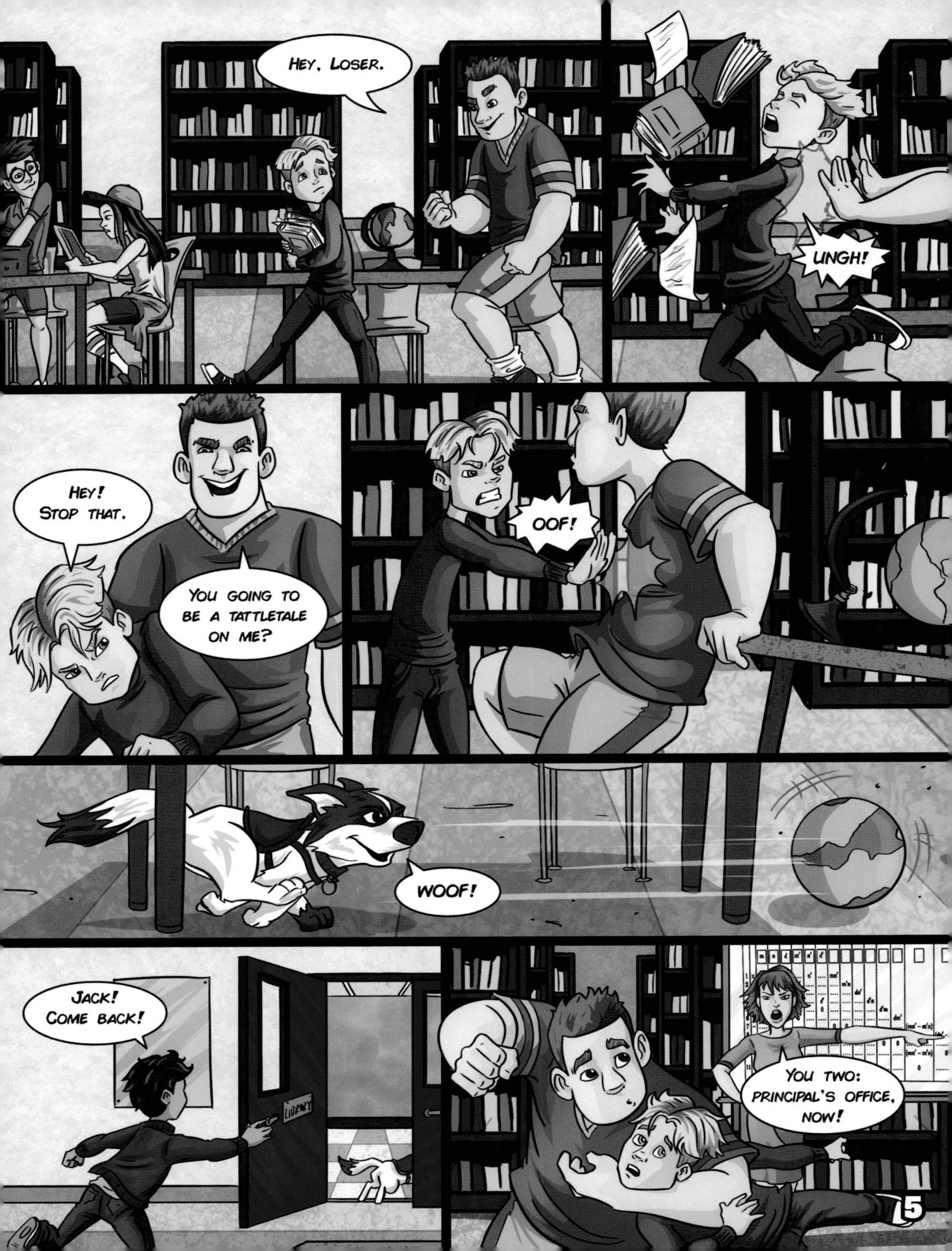
HEY, LOSER.
UNGH!
HEY! STOP THAT.
YOU GOING TO BE A TATTLETALE ON ME?
OOF!
WOOF!
JACK! COME BACK!
LIBRARY
YOU TWO: PRINCIPAL'S OFFICE, NOW!

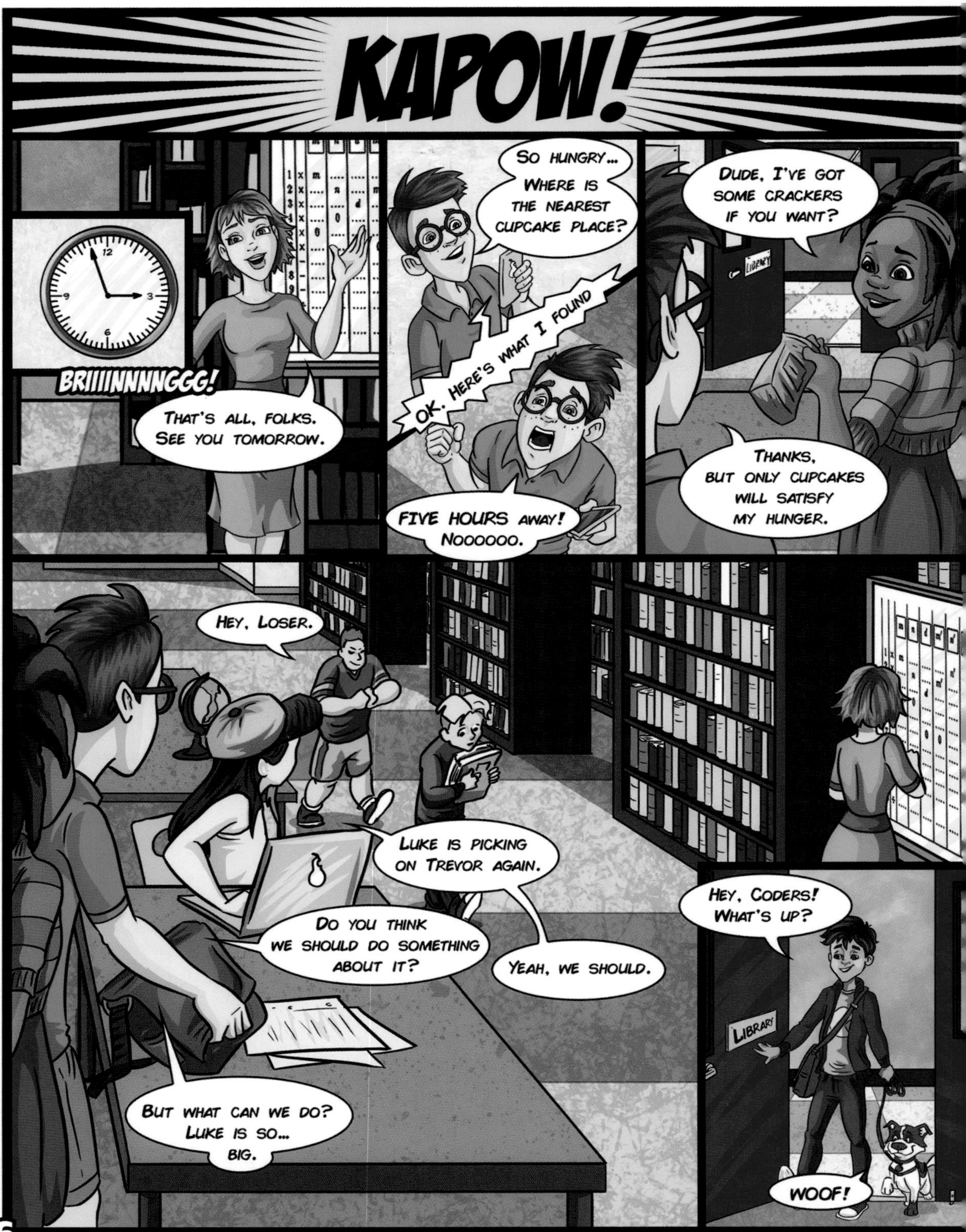
KAPOW!
BRIIIINNNNGGG!
THAT'S ALL, FOLKS. SEE YOU TOMORROW.
SO HUNGRY... WHERE IS THE NEAREST CUPCAKE PLACE?
OK. HERE'S WHAT I FOUND
FIVE HOURS AWAY! NOOOOOO.
DUDE, I'VE GOT SOME CRACKERS IF YOU WANT?
THANKS, BUT ONLY CUPCAKES WILL SATISFY MY HUNGER.
LIBRARY
HEY, LOSER.
LUKE IS PICKING ON TREVOR AGAIN.
DO YOU THINK WE SHOULD DO SOMETHING ABOUT IT?
YEAH, WE SHOULD.
BUT WHAT CAN WE DO? LUKE IS SO... BIG.
HEY, CODERS! WHAT'S UP?
LIBRARY
WOOF!

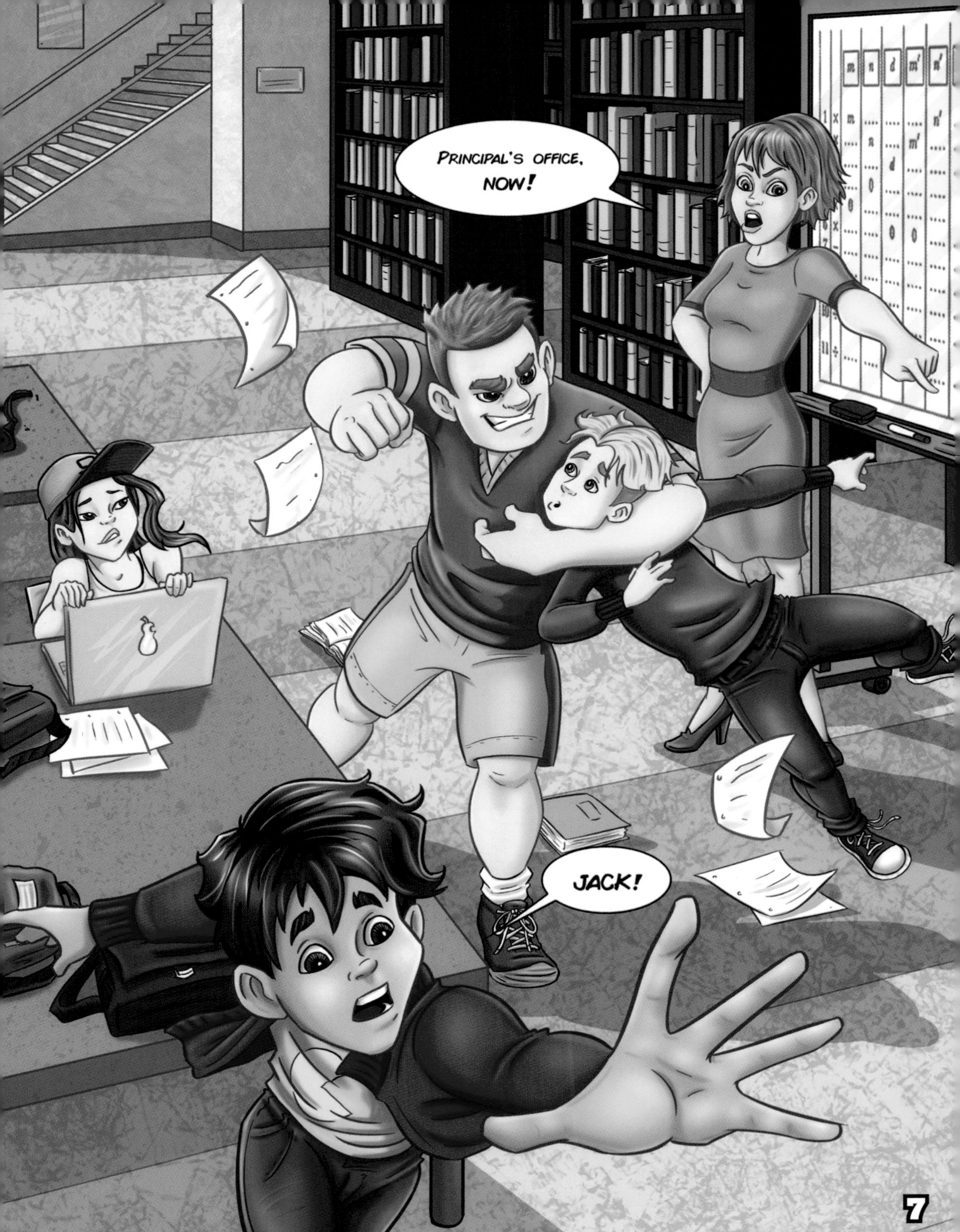
PRINCIPAL'S OFFICE, NOW!
JACK!

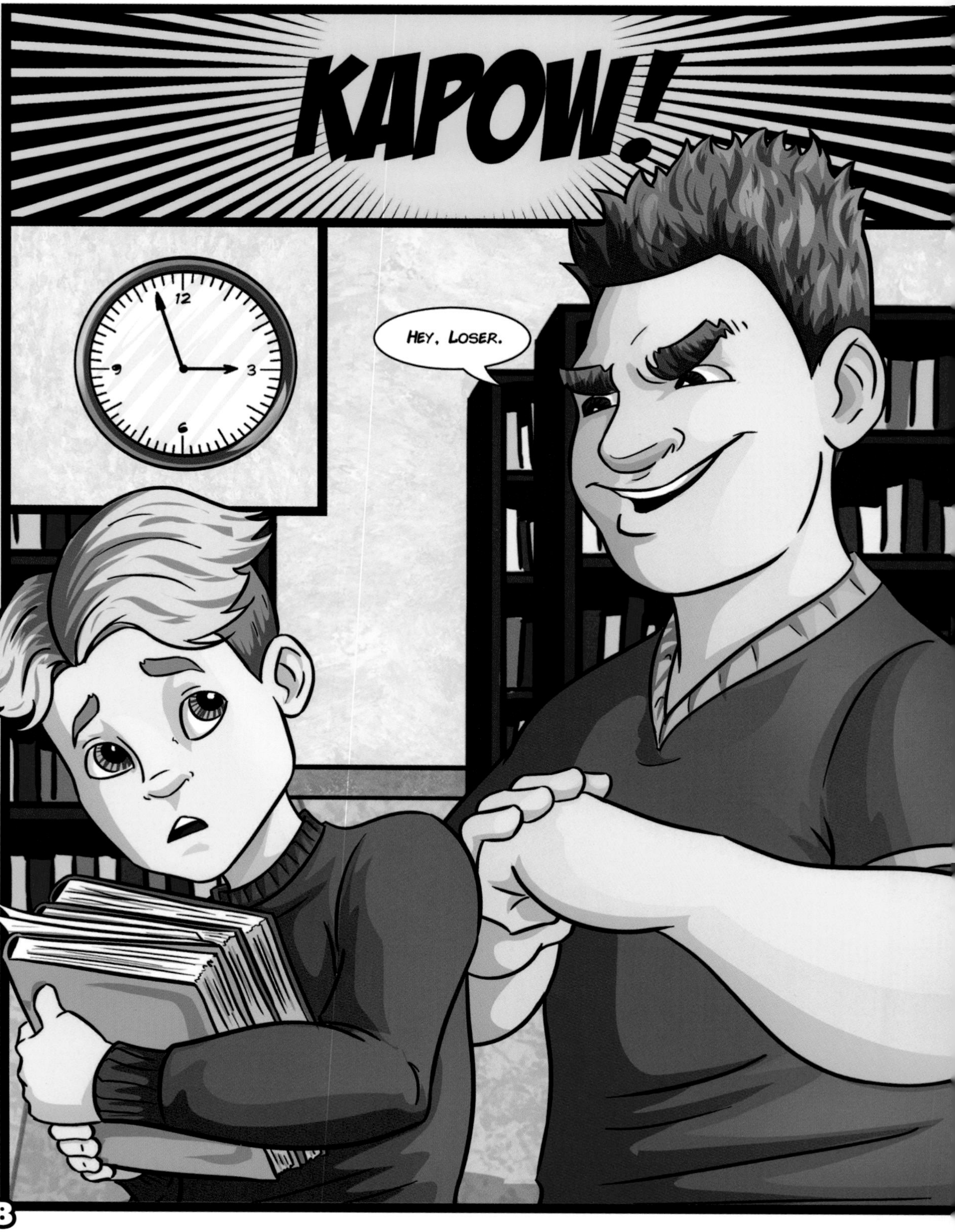
KAPOW!
HEY, LOSER.

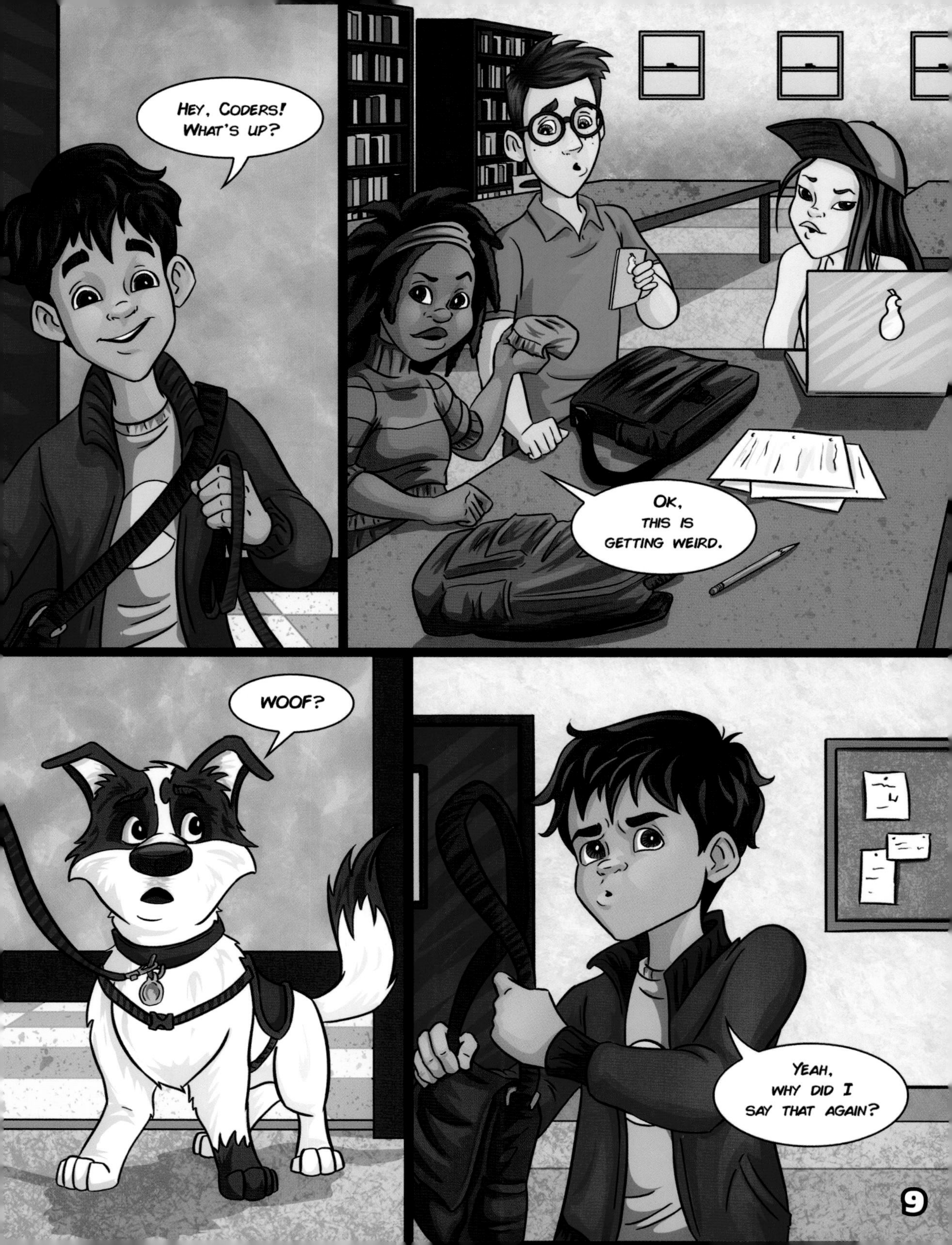
HEY, CODERS! WHAT'S UP?
OK, THIS IS GETTING WEIRD.
WOOF?
YEAH, WHY DID I SAY THAT AGAIN?

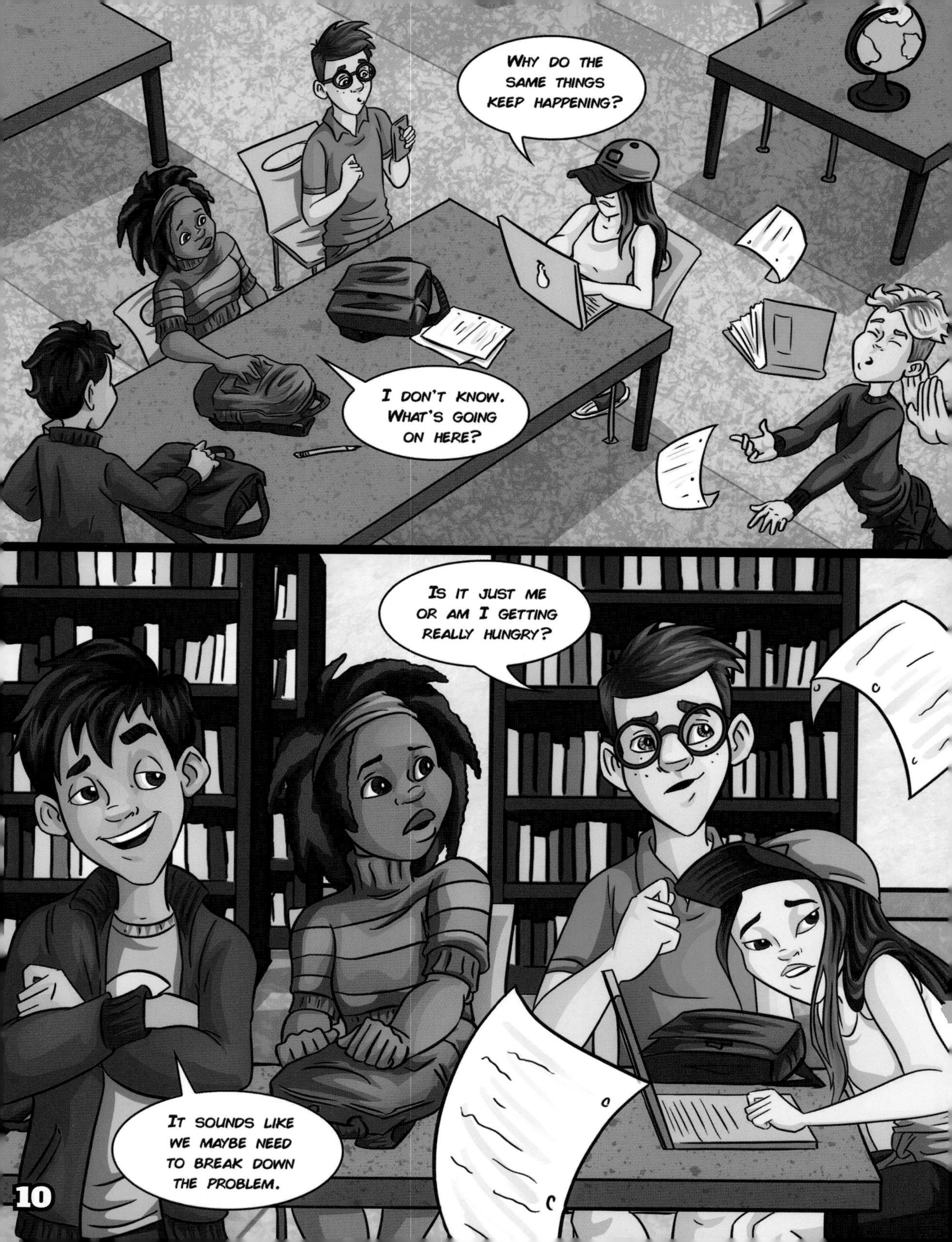
WHY DO THE SAME THINGS KEEP HAPPENING?
I DON'T KNOW. WHAT'S GOING ON HERE?
IS IT JUST ME OR AM I GETTING REALLY HUNGRY?
IT SOUNDS LIKE WE MAYBE NEED TO BREAK DOWN THE PROBLEM.

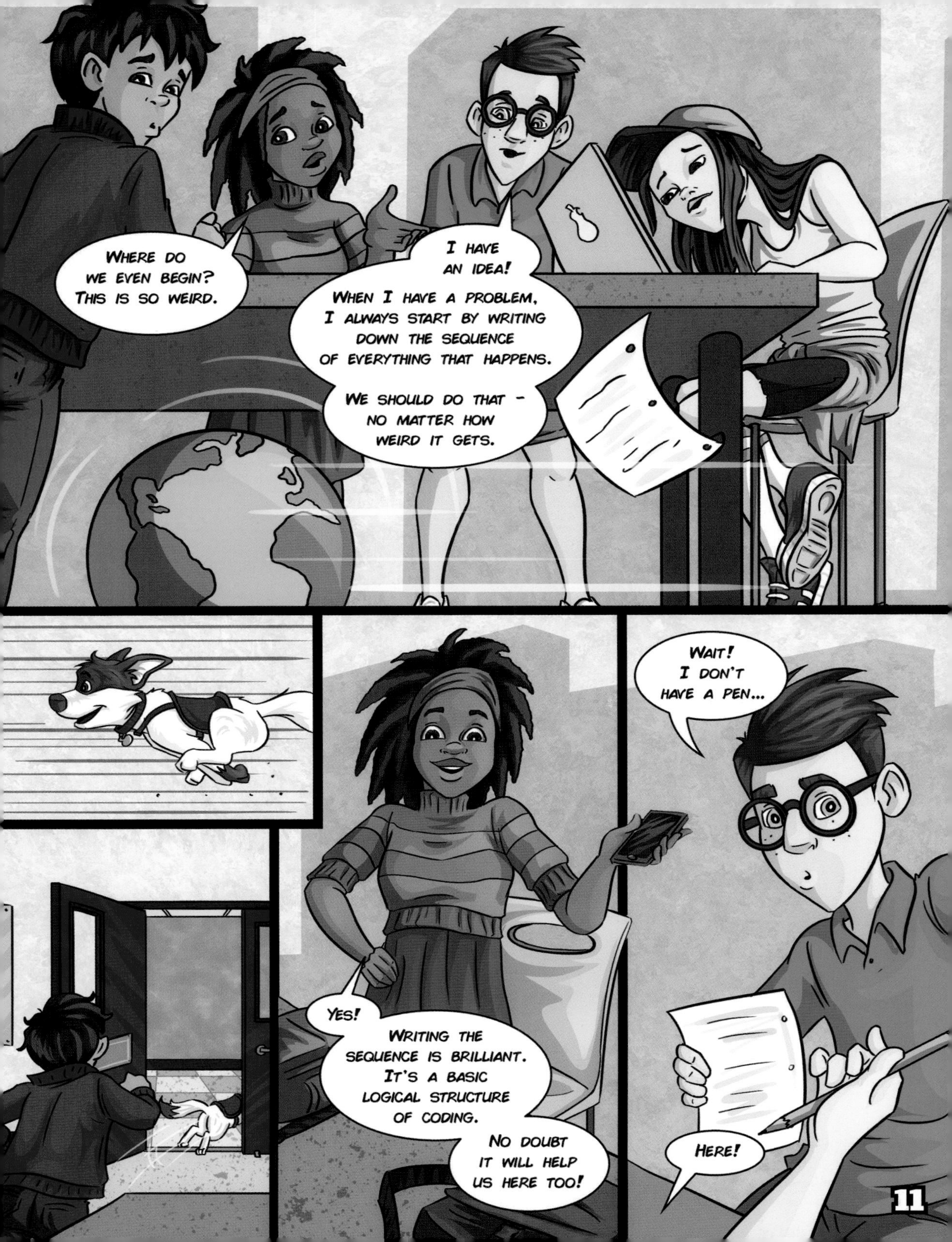

WHERE DO WE EVEN BEGIN? THIS IS SO WEIRD.
I HAVE AN IDEA!
WHEN I HAVE A PROBLEM, I ALWAYS START BY WRITING DOWN THE SEQUENCE OF EVERYTHING THAT HAPPENS.
WE SHOULD DO THAT - NO MATTER HOW WEIRD IT GETS.
YES!
WRITING THE SEQUENCE IS BRILLIANT. IT'S A BASIC LOGICAL STRUCTURE OF CODING.
NO DOUBT IT WILL HELP US HERE TOO!
WAIT! I DON'T HAVE A PEN...
HERE!

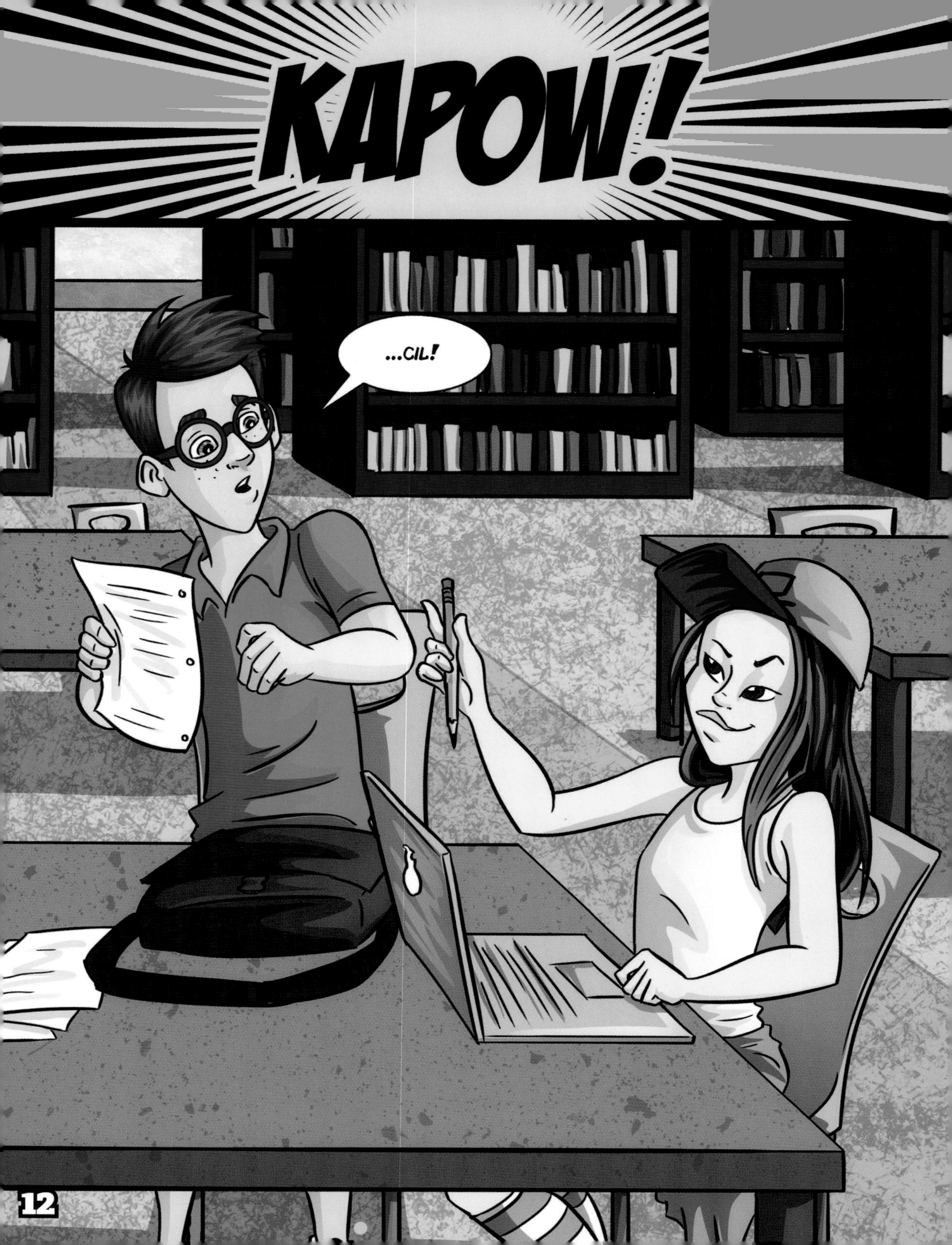
KAPOW!
...CIL!

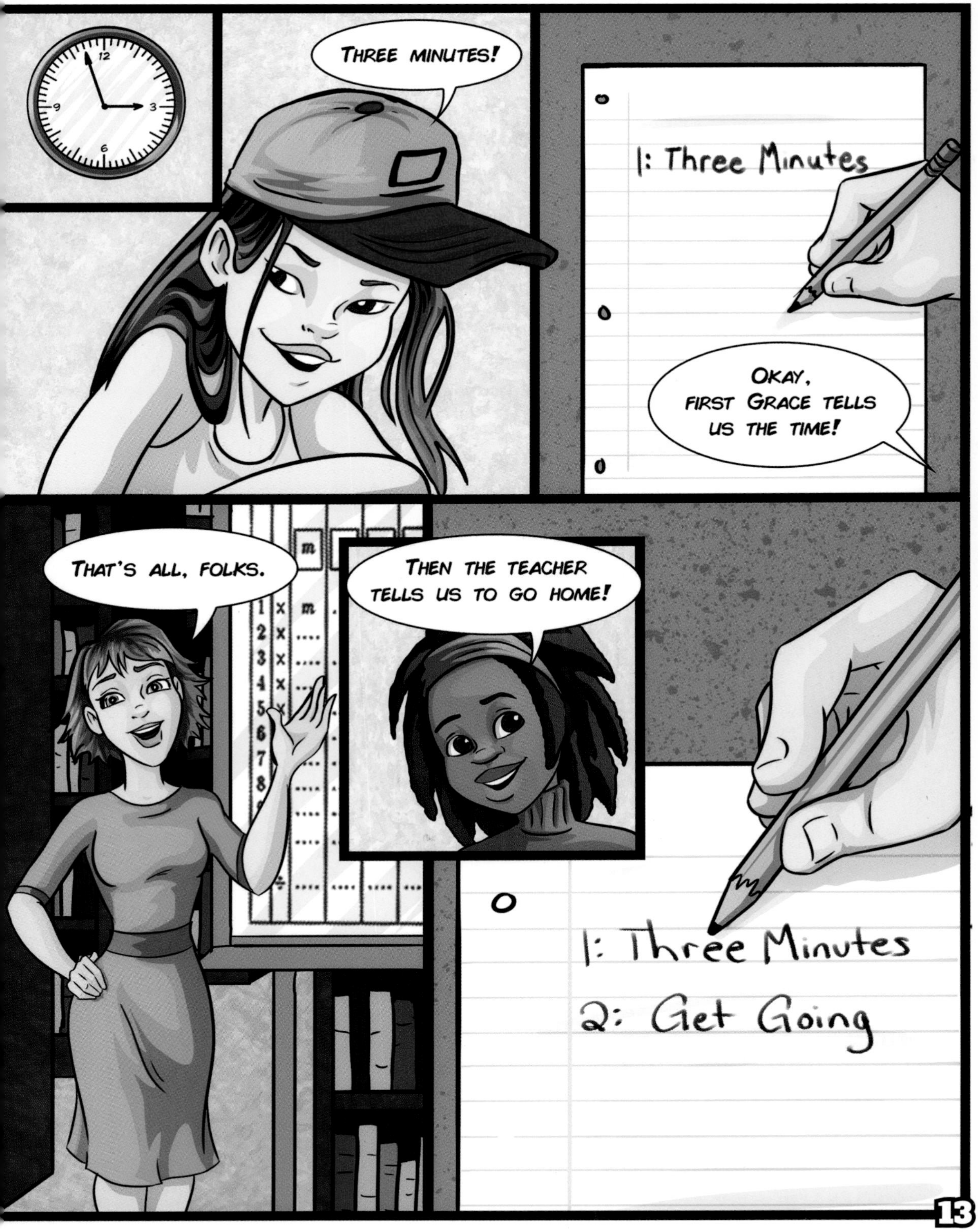
THREE MINUTES!
1: Three Minutes
OKAY, FIRST GRACE TELLS US THE TIME!
THAT'S ALL, FOLKS.
THEN THE TEACHER TELLS US TO GO HOME!
1: Three Minutes
2: Get Going

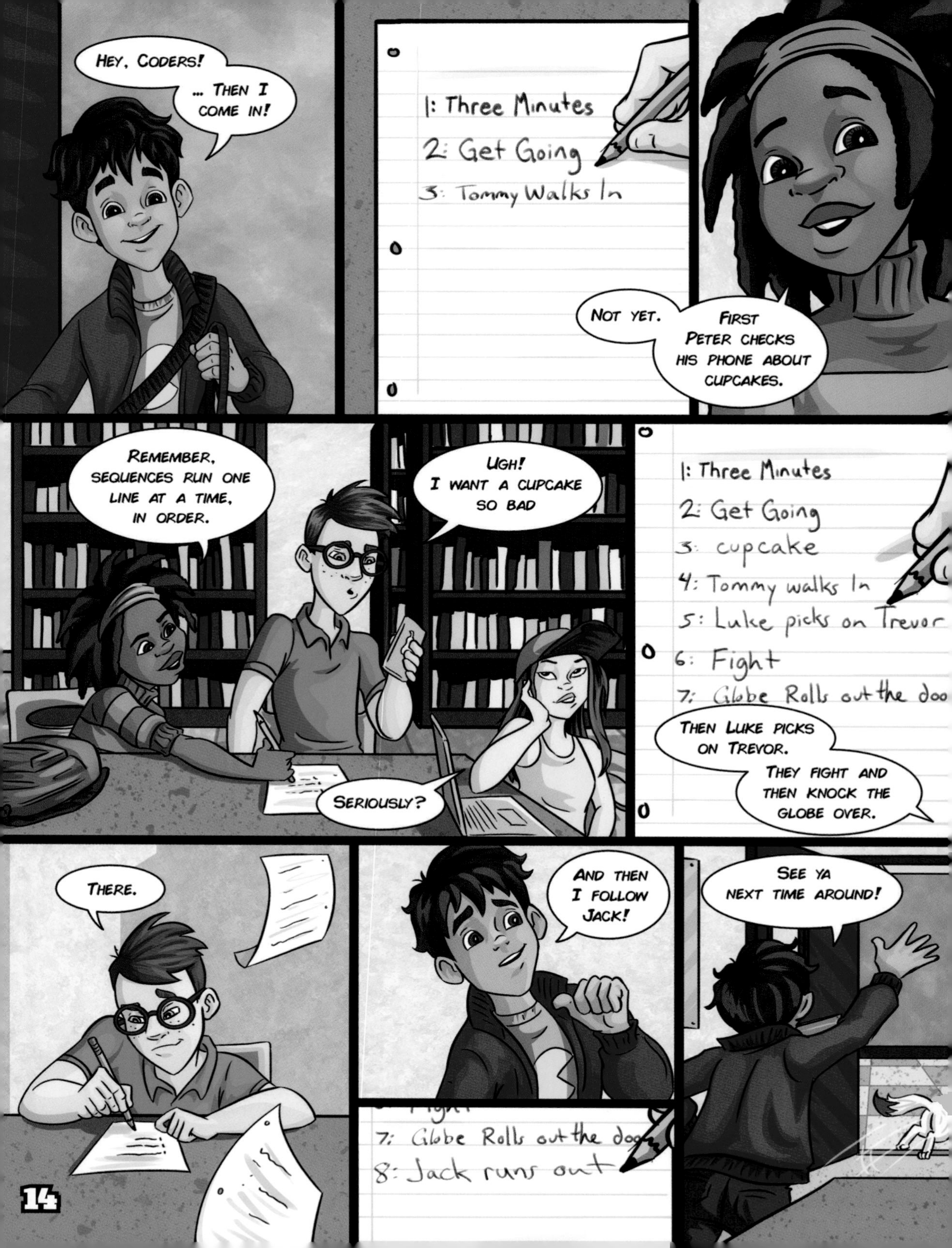
HEY, CODERS!
... THEN I COME IN!
1: Three Minutes
2: Get Going
3: Tommy Walks In
NOT YET.
FIRST PETER CHECKS HIS PHONE ABOUT CUPCAKES.
REMEMBER, SEQUENCES RUN ONE LINE AT A TIME, IN ORDER.
UGH! I WANT A CUPCAKE SO BAD
SERIOUSLY?
1: Three Minutes
2: Get Going
3: cupcake
4: Tommy walks In
5: Luke picks on Trevor
6: Fight
7: Globe Rolls out the doo
THEN LUKE PICKS ON TREVOR.
THEY FIGHT AND THEN KNOCK THE GLOBE OVER.
THERE.
AND THEN I FOLLOW JACK!
7: Globe Rolls out the do
8: Jack runs out
SEE YA NEXT TIME AROUND!

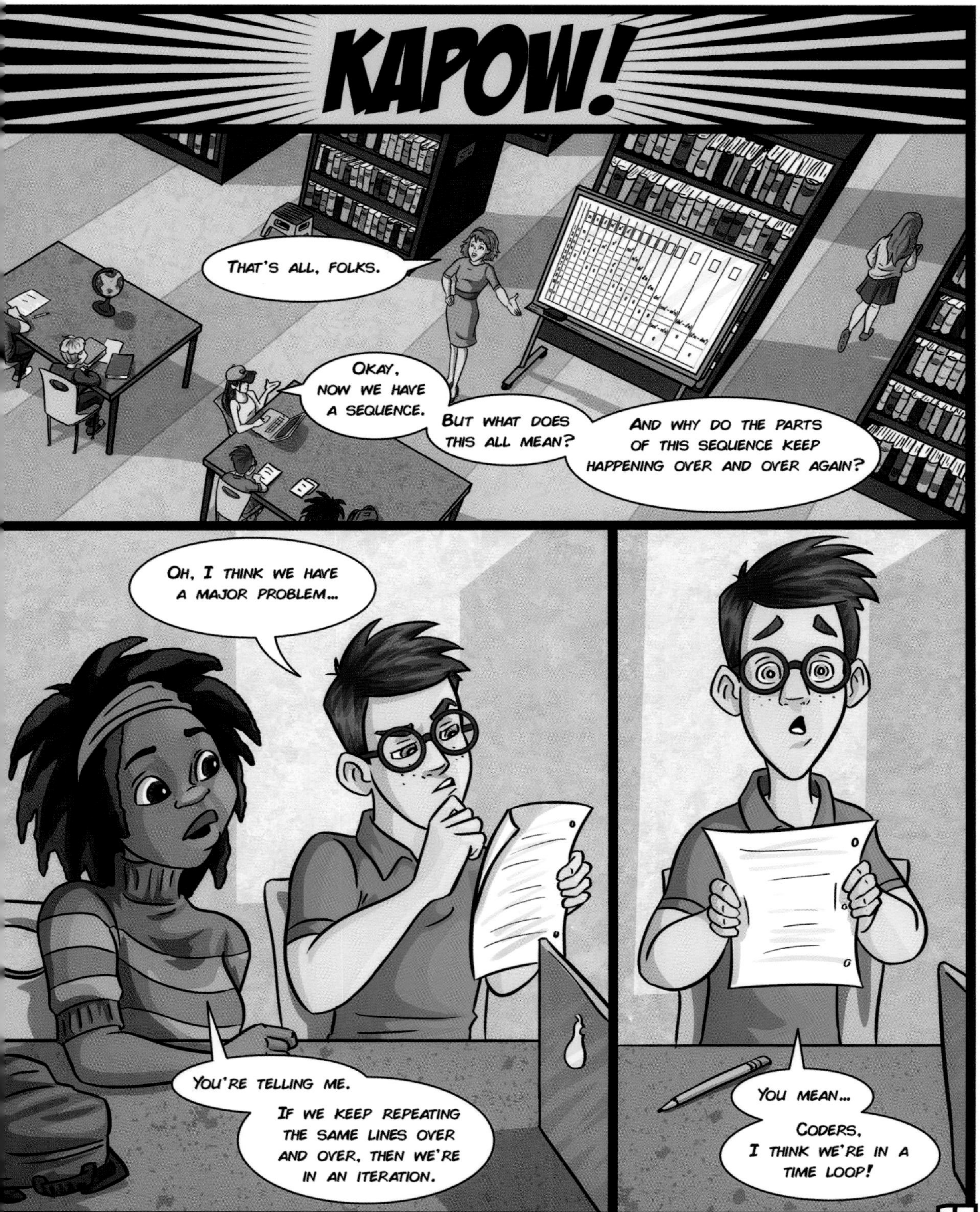
KAPOW!
THAT'S ALL, FOLKS.
OKAY, NOW WE HAVE A SEQUENCE.
BUT WHAT DOES THIS ALL MEAN?
AND WHY DO THE PARTS OF THIS SEQUENCE KEEP HAPPENING OVER AND OVER AGAIN?
OH, I THINK WE HAVE A MAJOR PROBLEM...
YOU'RE TELLING ME.
IF WE KEEP REPEATING THE SAME LINES OVER AND OVER, THEN WE'RE IN AN ITERATION.
YOU MEAN...
CODERS, I THINK WE'RE IN A TIME LOOP!

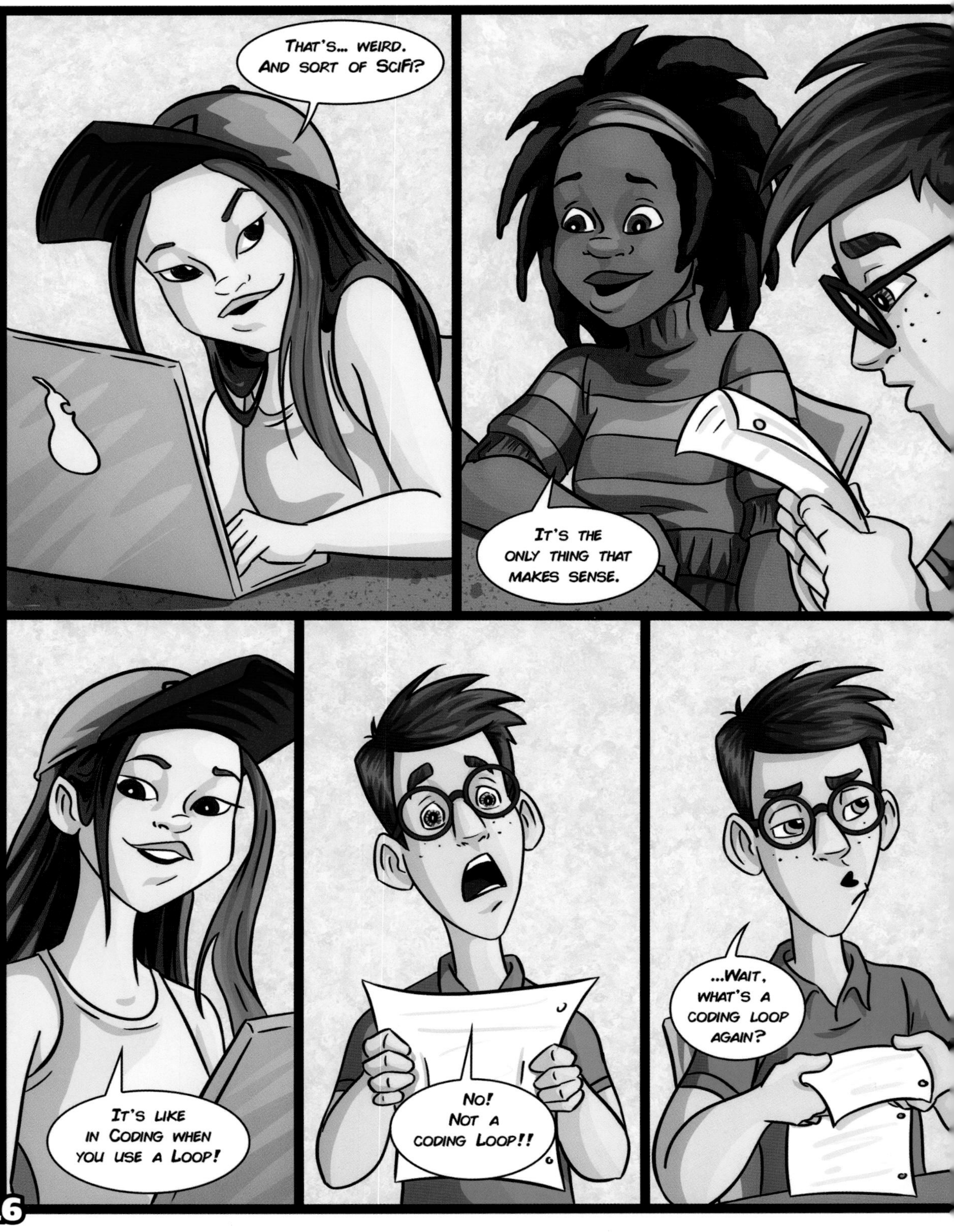
THAT'S... WEIRD. AND SORT OF SCIFI?
IT'S THE ONLY THING THAT MAKES SENSE.
IT'S LIKE IN CODING WHEN YOU USE A LOOP!
NO! NOT A CODING LOOP!!
...WAIT, WHAT'S A CODING LOOP AGAIN?

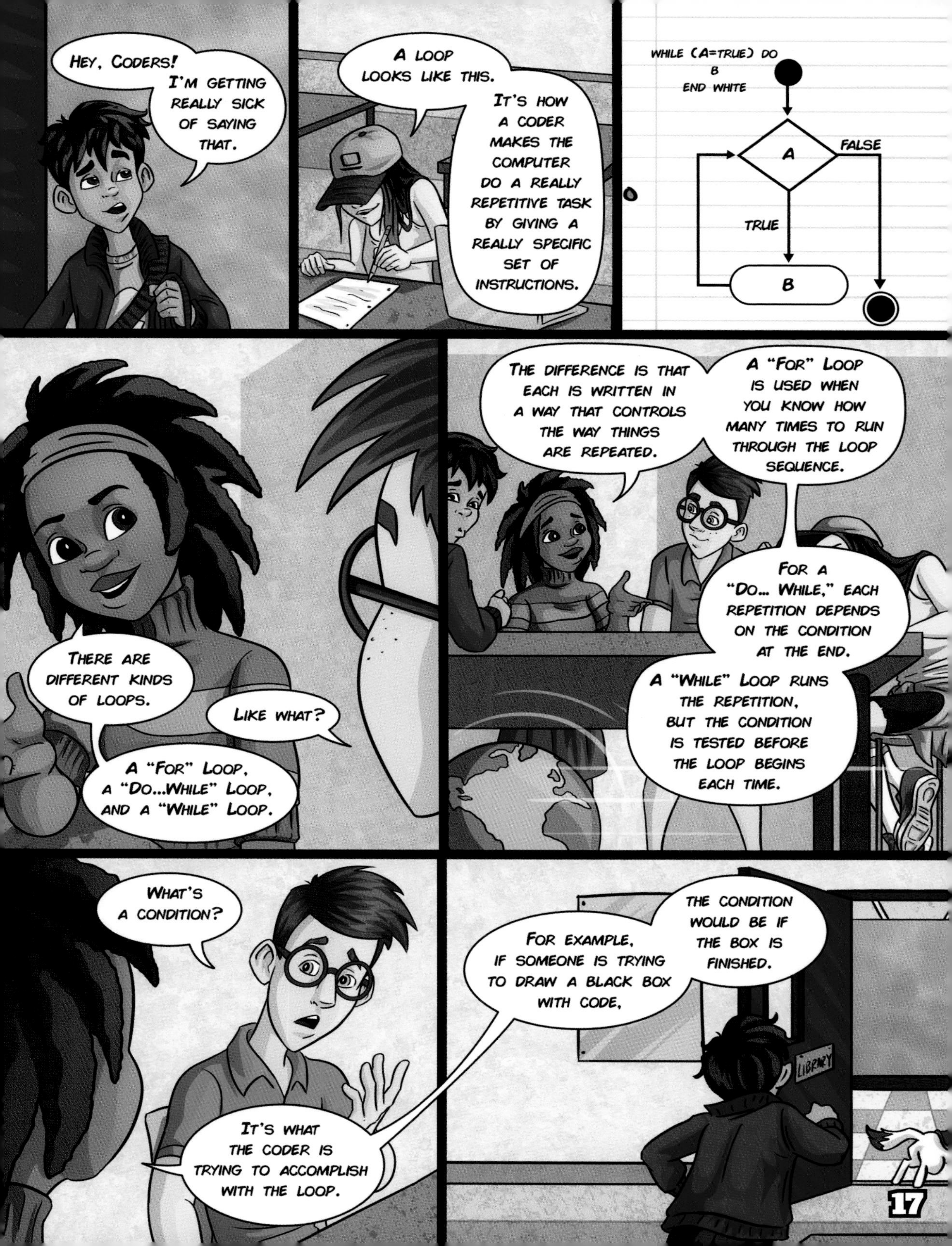
HEY, CODERS!
I'M GETTING REALLY SICK OF SAYING THAT.
A LOOP LOOKS LIKE THIS.
IT'S HOW A CODER MAKES THE COMPUTER DO A REALLY REPETITIVE TASK BY GIVING A REALLY SPECIFIC SET OF INSTRUCTIONS.
WHILE (A=TRUE) DO
B
END WHITE
A
FALSE
TRUE
B
THERE ARE DIFFERENT KINDS OF LOOPS.
LIKE WHAT?
A "FOR" LOOP, A "DO...WHILE" LOOP, AND A "WHILE" LOOP.
THE DIFFERENCE IS THAT EACH IS WRITTEN IN A WAY THAT CONTROLS THE WAY THINGS ARE REPEATED.
A "FOR" LOOP IS USED WHEN YOU KNOW HOW MANY TIMES TO RUN THROUGH THE LOOP SEQUENCE.
FOR A "DO... WHILE," EACH REPETITION DEPENDS ON THE CONDITION AT THE END.
A "WHILE" LOOP RUNS THE REPETITION, BUT THE CONDITION IS TESTED BEFORE THE LOOP BEGINS EACH TIME.
WHAT'S A CONDITION?
IT'S WHAT THE CODER IS TRYING TO ACCOMPLISH WITH THE LOOP.
FOR EXAMPLE, IF SOMEONE IS TRYING TO DRAW A BLACK BOX WITH CODE,
THE CONDITION WOULD BE IF THE BOX IS FINISHED.
LIBRARY

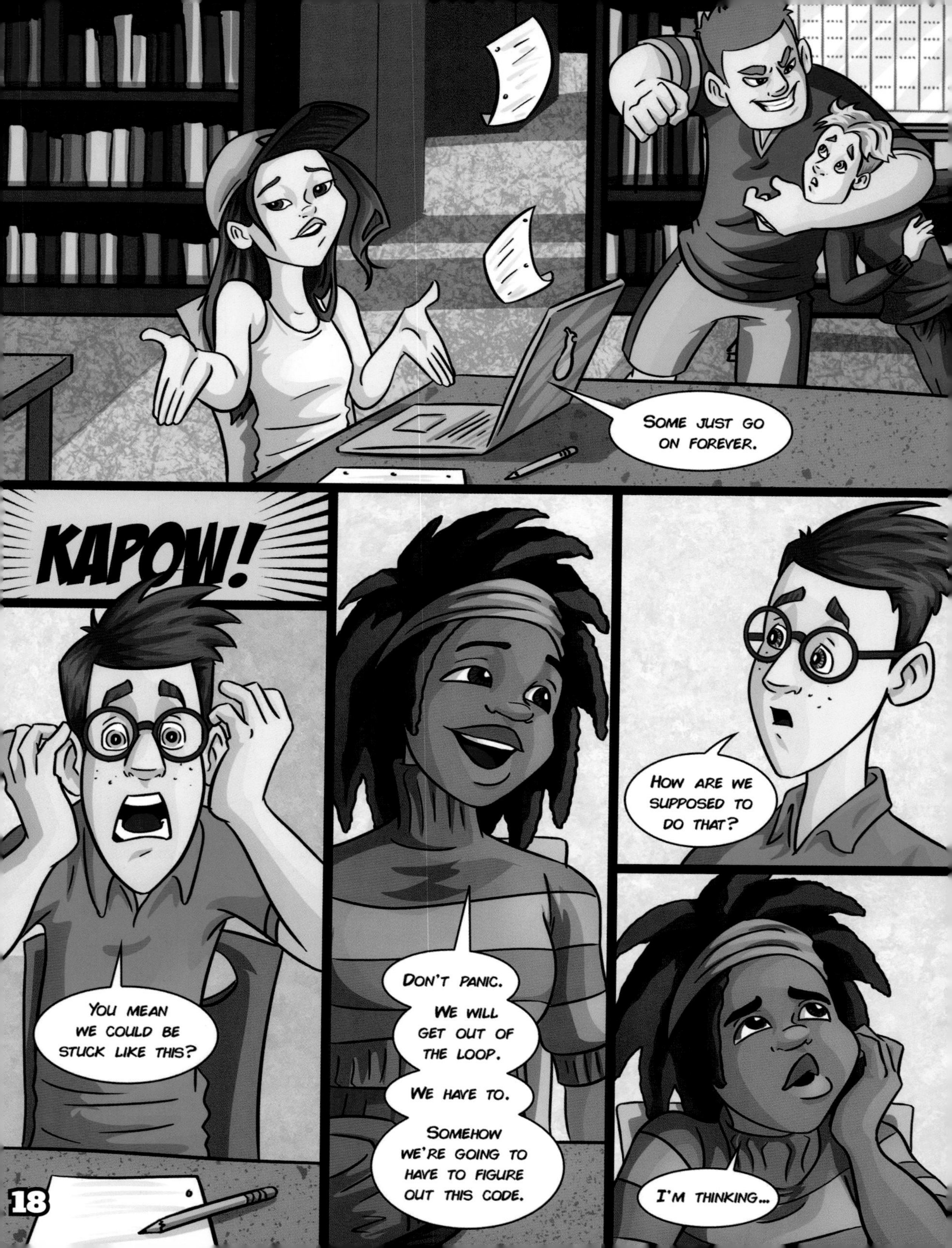
SOME JUST GO ON FOREVER.
KAPOW!
YOU MEAN WE COULD BE STUCK LIKE THIS?
DON'T PANIC.
WE WILL GET OUT OF THE LOOP.
WE HAVE TO.
SOMEHOW WE'RE GOING TO HAVE TO FIGURE OUT THIS CODE.
HOW ARE WE SUPPOSED TO DO THAT?
I'M THINKING...

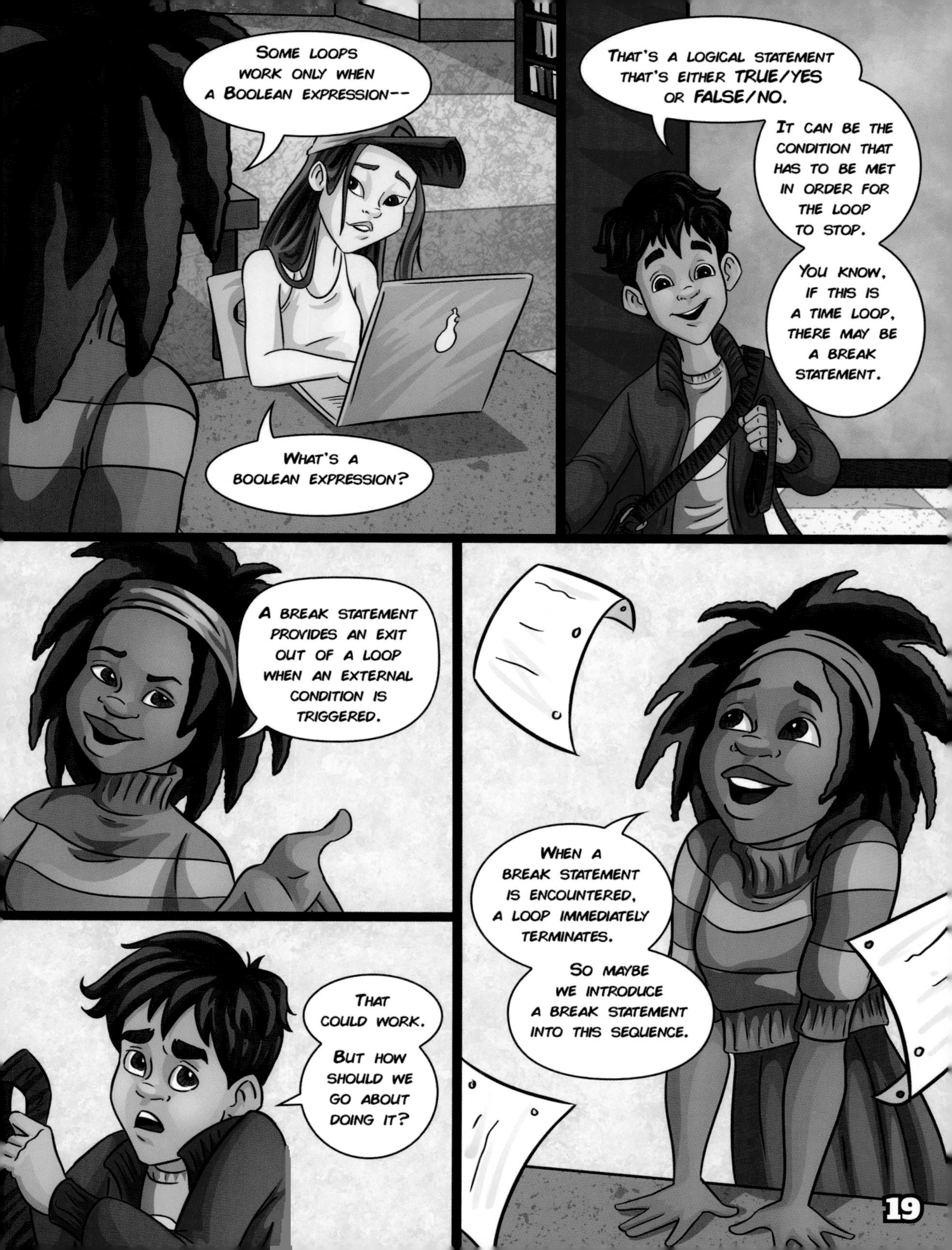
SOME LOOPS WORK ONLY WHEN A BOOLEAN EXPRESSION--
WHAT'S A BOOLEAN EXPRESSION?
THAT'S A LOGICAL STATEMENT THAT'S EITHER TRUE/YES OR FALSE/NO.
IT CAN BE THE CONDITION THAT HAS TO BE MET IN ORDER FOR THE LOOP TO STOP.
YOU KNOW, IF THIS IS A TIME LOOP, THERE MAY BE A BREAK STATEMENT.
A BREAK STATEMENT PROVIDES AN EXIT OUT OF A LOOP WHEN AN EXTERNAL CONDITION IS TRIGGERED.
WHEN A BREAK STATEMENT IS ENCOUNTERED, A LOOP IMMEDIATELY TERMINATES.
SO MAYBE WE INTRODUCE A BREAK STATEMENT INTO THIS SEQUENCE.
THAT COULD WORK.
BUT HOW SHOULD WE GO ABOUT DOING IT?

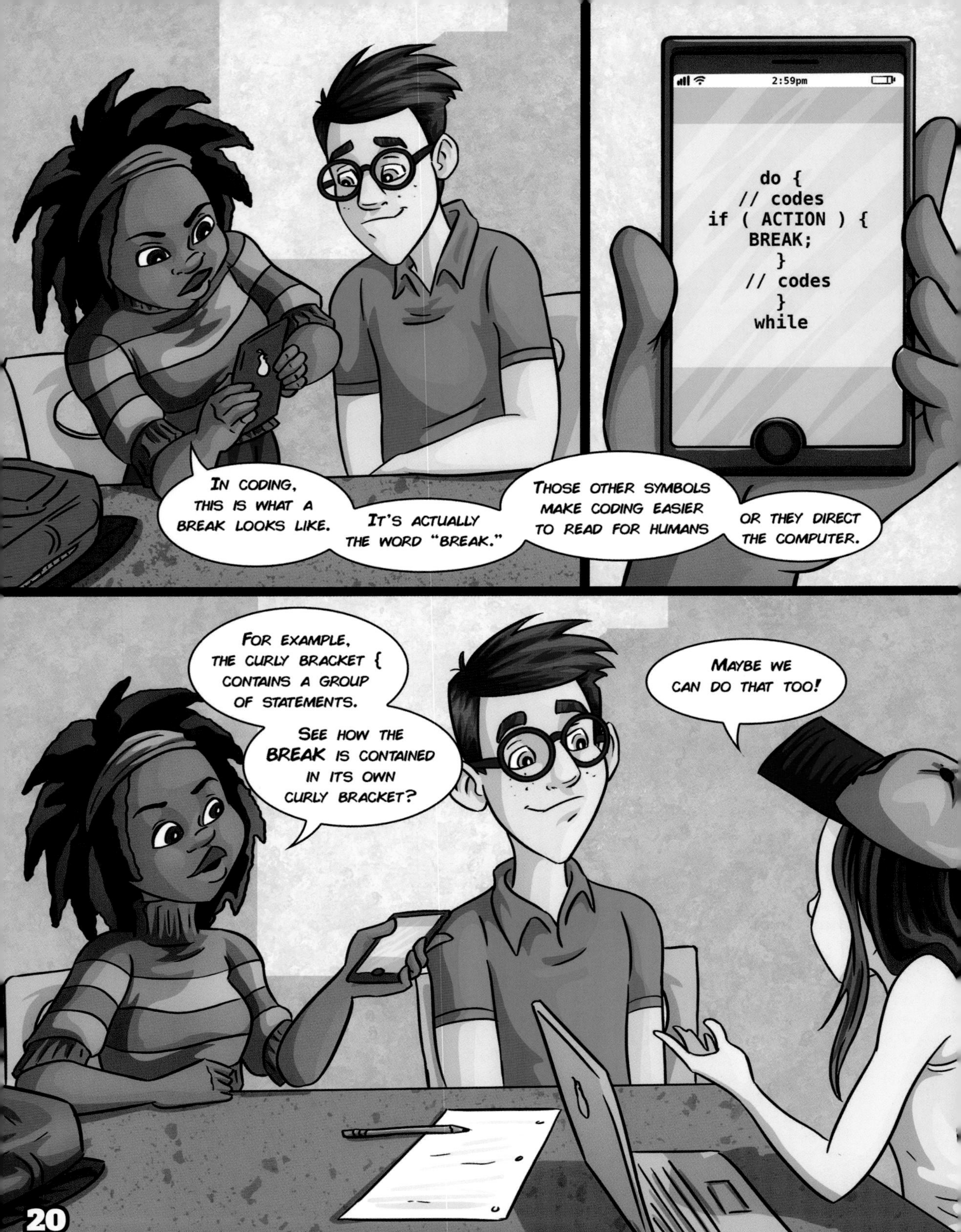
2:59pm
do {
// codes
if (ACTION) {
BREAK;
}
// codes
}
while
IN CODING, THIS IS WHAT A BREAK LOOKS LIKE.
IT'S ACTUALLY THE WORD "BREAK."
THOSE OTHER SYMBOLS MAKE CODING EASIER TO READ FOR HUMANS
OR THEY DIRECT THE COMPUTER.
FOR EXAMPLE, THE CURLY BRACKET { CONTAINS A GROUP OF STATEMENTS.
SEE HOW THE BREAK IS CONTAINED IN ITS OWN CURLY BRACKET?
MAYBE WE CAN DO THAT TOO!

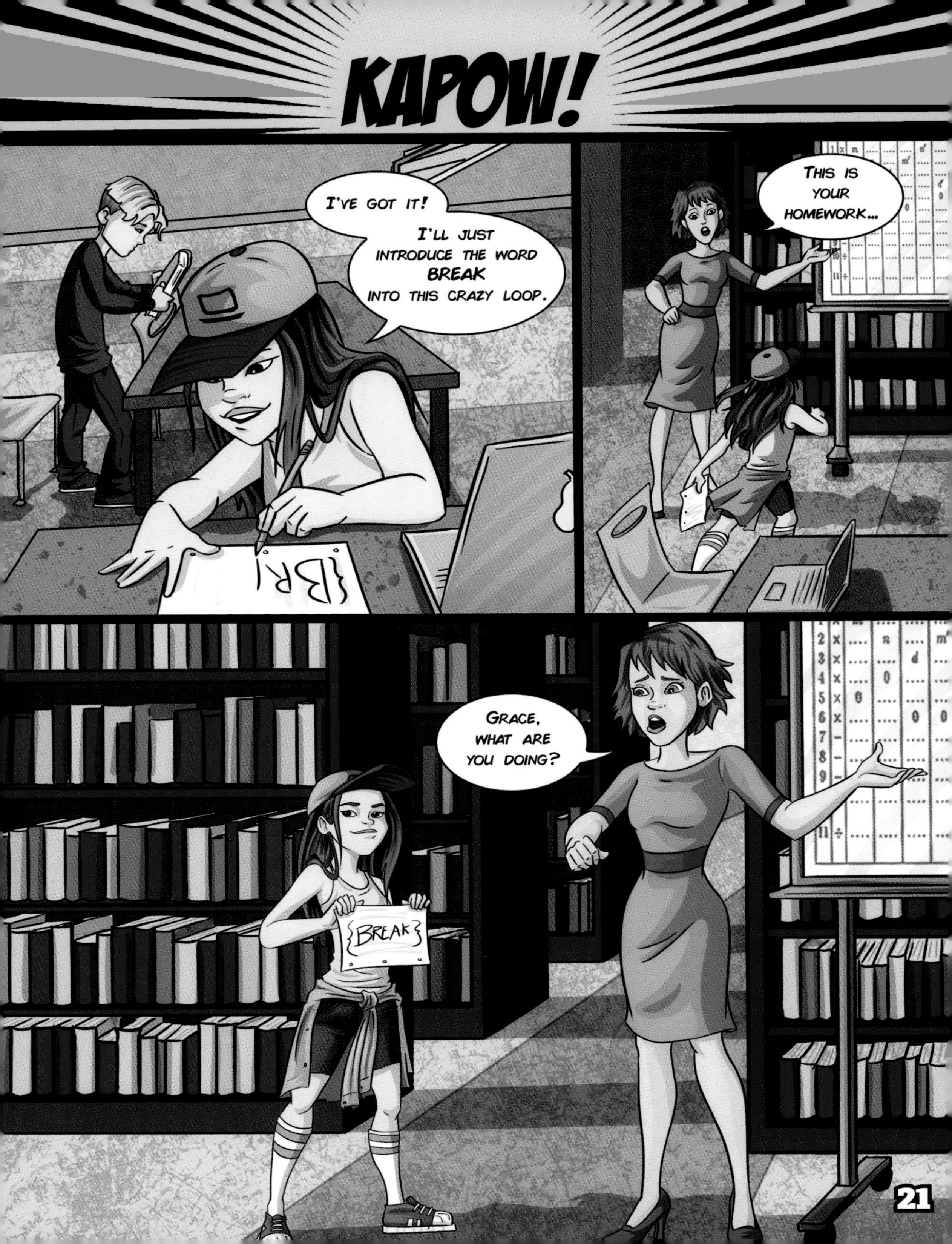
KAPOW!
I'VE GOT IT!
I'LL JUST INTRODUCE THE WORD BREAK INTO THIS CRAZY LOOP.
THIS IS YOUR HOMEWORK...
GRACE, WHAT ARE YOU DOING?
{BREAK}

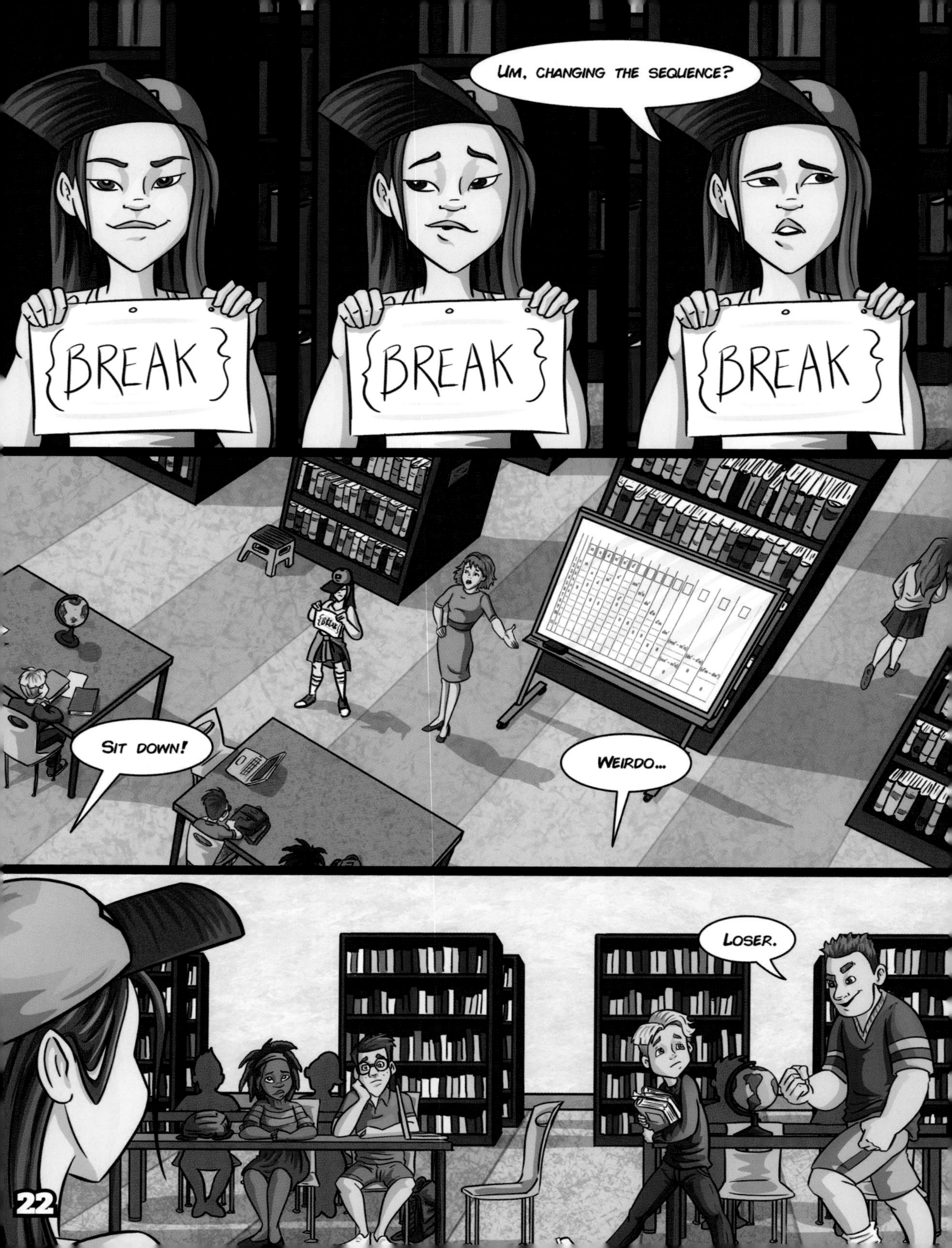
{BREAK}
{BREAK}
UM, CHANGING THE SEQUENCE?
{BREAK}
SIT DOWN!
WEIRDO...
LOSER.

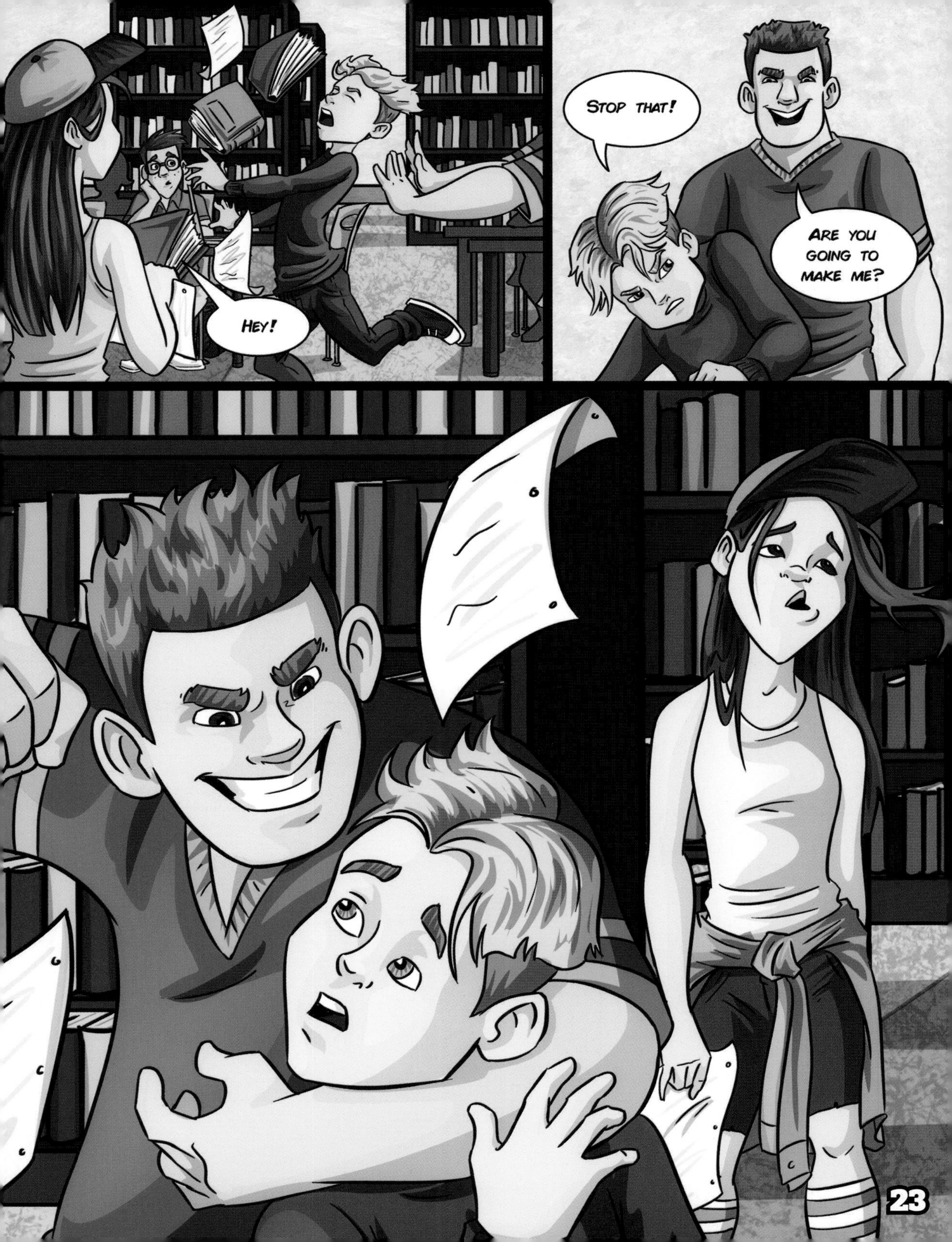
HEY!
STOP THAT!
ARE YOU GOING TO MAKE ME?

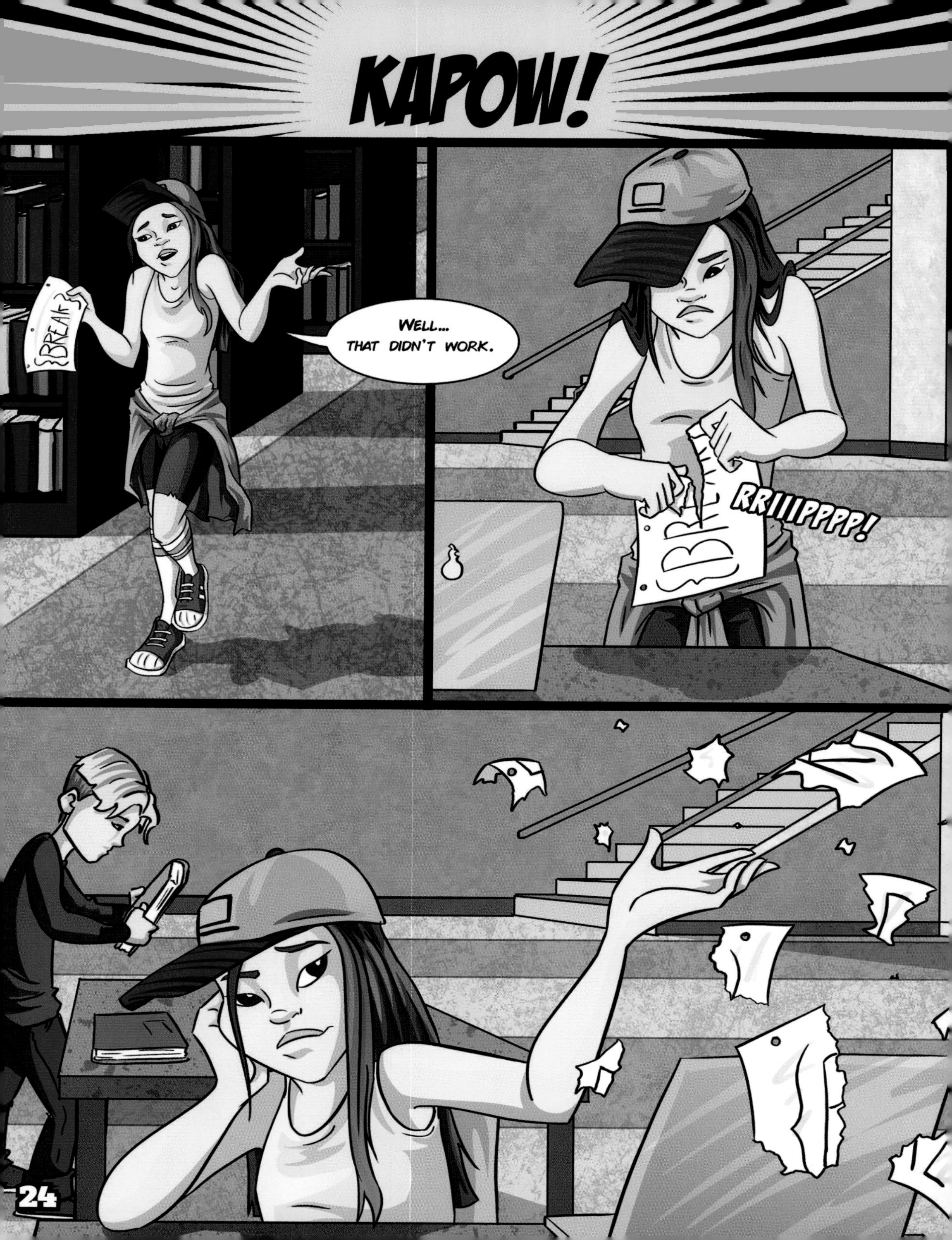
KAPOW!
BREAK
WELL... THAT DIDN'T WORK.
RRIIIPPPP!

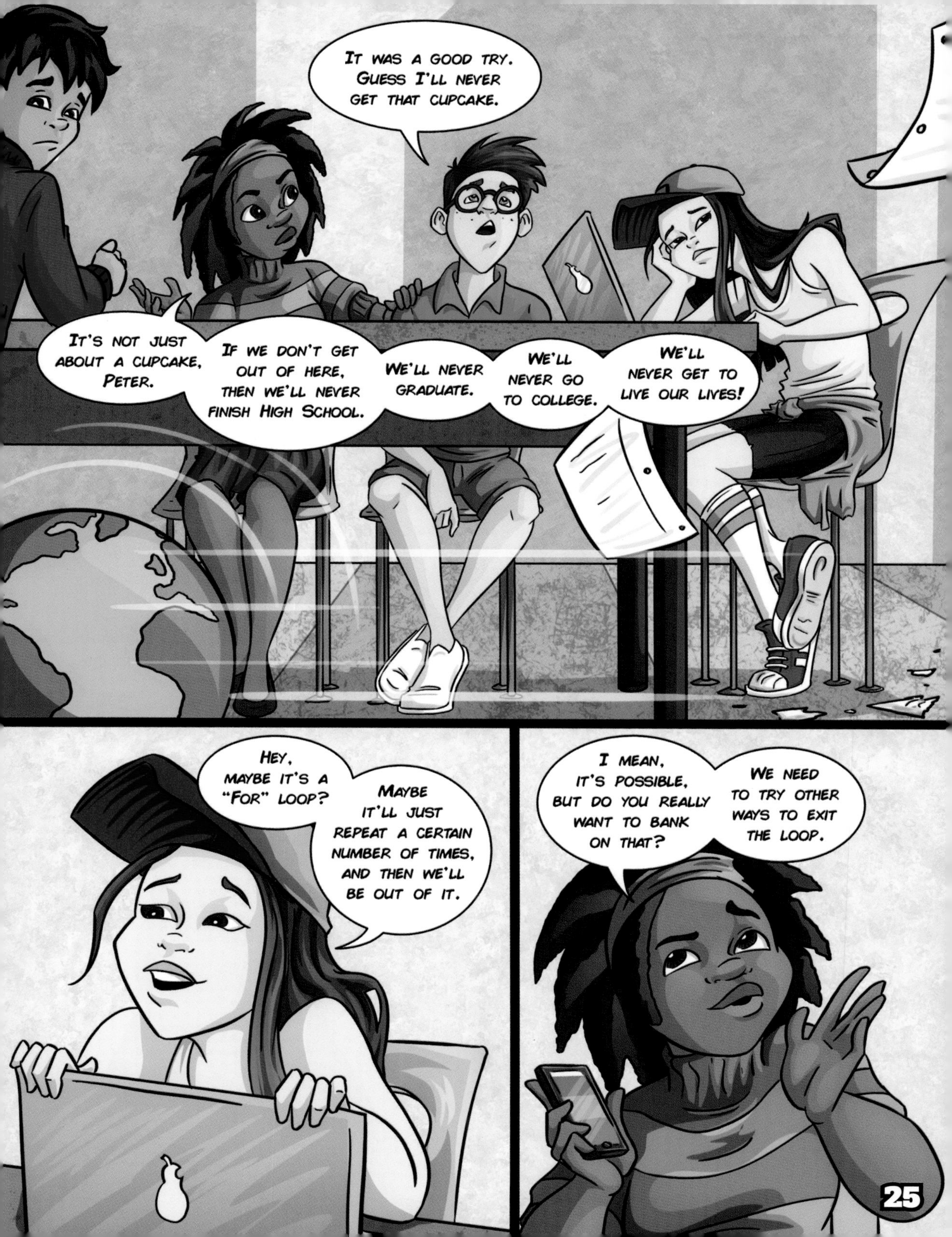

It was a good try. Guess I'll never get that cupcake.
It's not just about a cupcake, Peter.
If we don't get out of here, then we'll never finish High School.
We'll never graduate.
We'll never go to college.
We'll never get to live our lives!
Hey, maybe it's a "For" loop?
Maybe it'll just repeat a certain number of times, and then we'll be out of it.
I mean, it's possible, but do you really want to bank on that?
We need to try other ways to exit the loop.

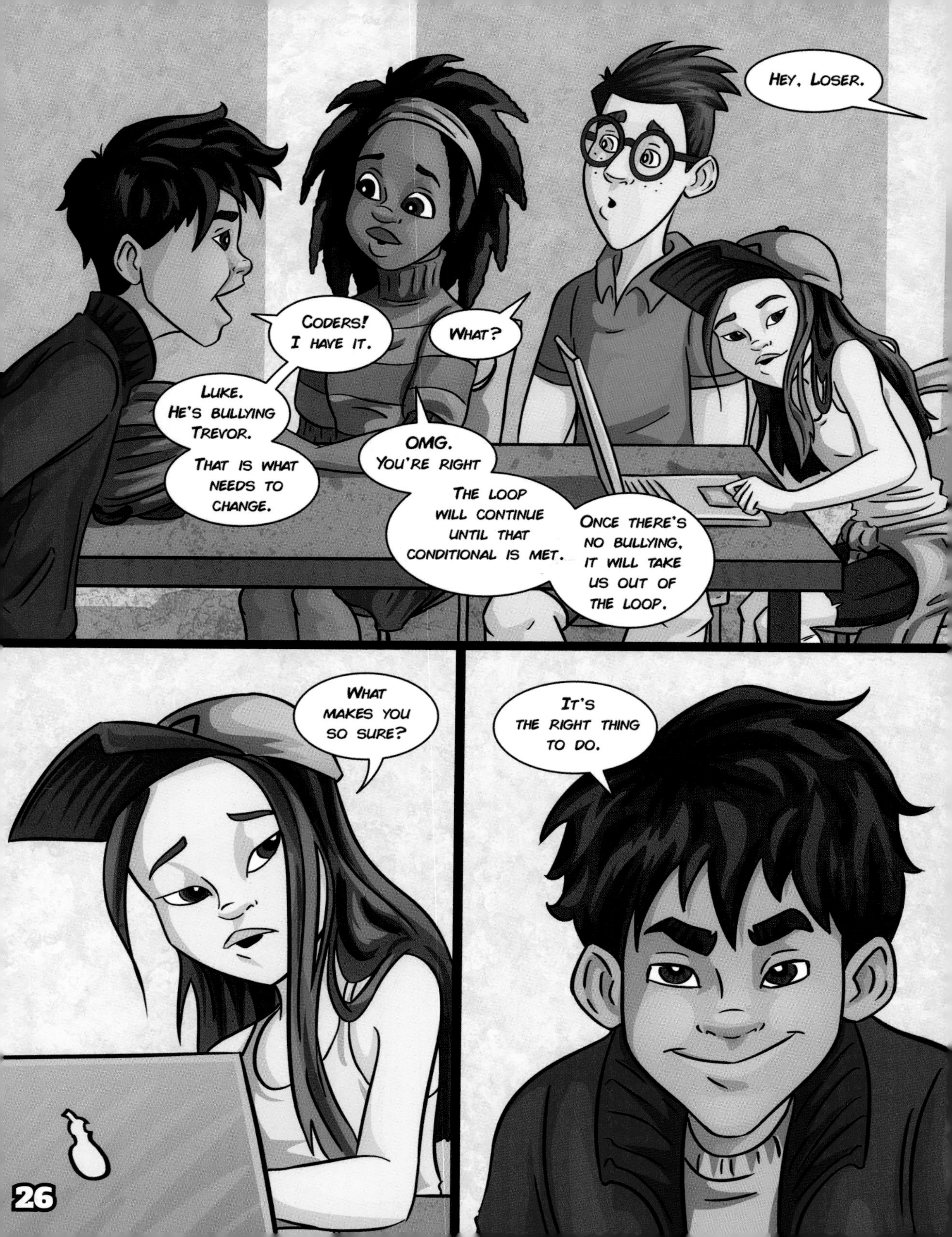
Hey, Loser.
Coders! I have it.
What?
Luke. He's bullying Trevor.
That is what needs to change.
OMG. You're right
The loop will continue until that conditional is met.
Once there's no bullying, it will take us out of the loop.
What makes you so sure?
It's the right thing to do.

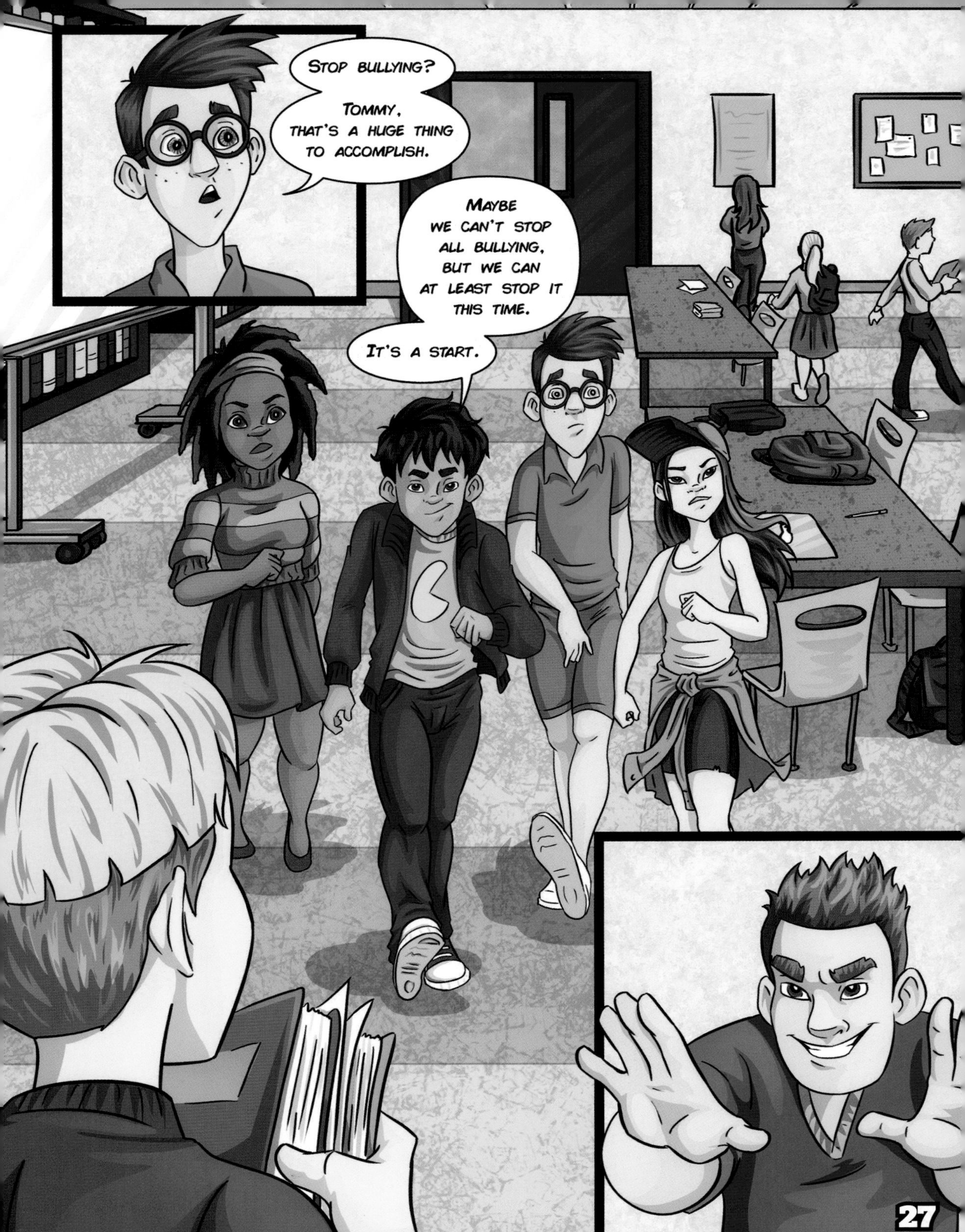

STOP BULLYING?
TOMMY, THAT'S A HUGE THING TO ACCOMPLISH.
MAYBE WE CAN'T STOP ALL BULLYING, BUT WE CAN AT LEAST STOP IT THIS TIME.
IT'S A START.

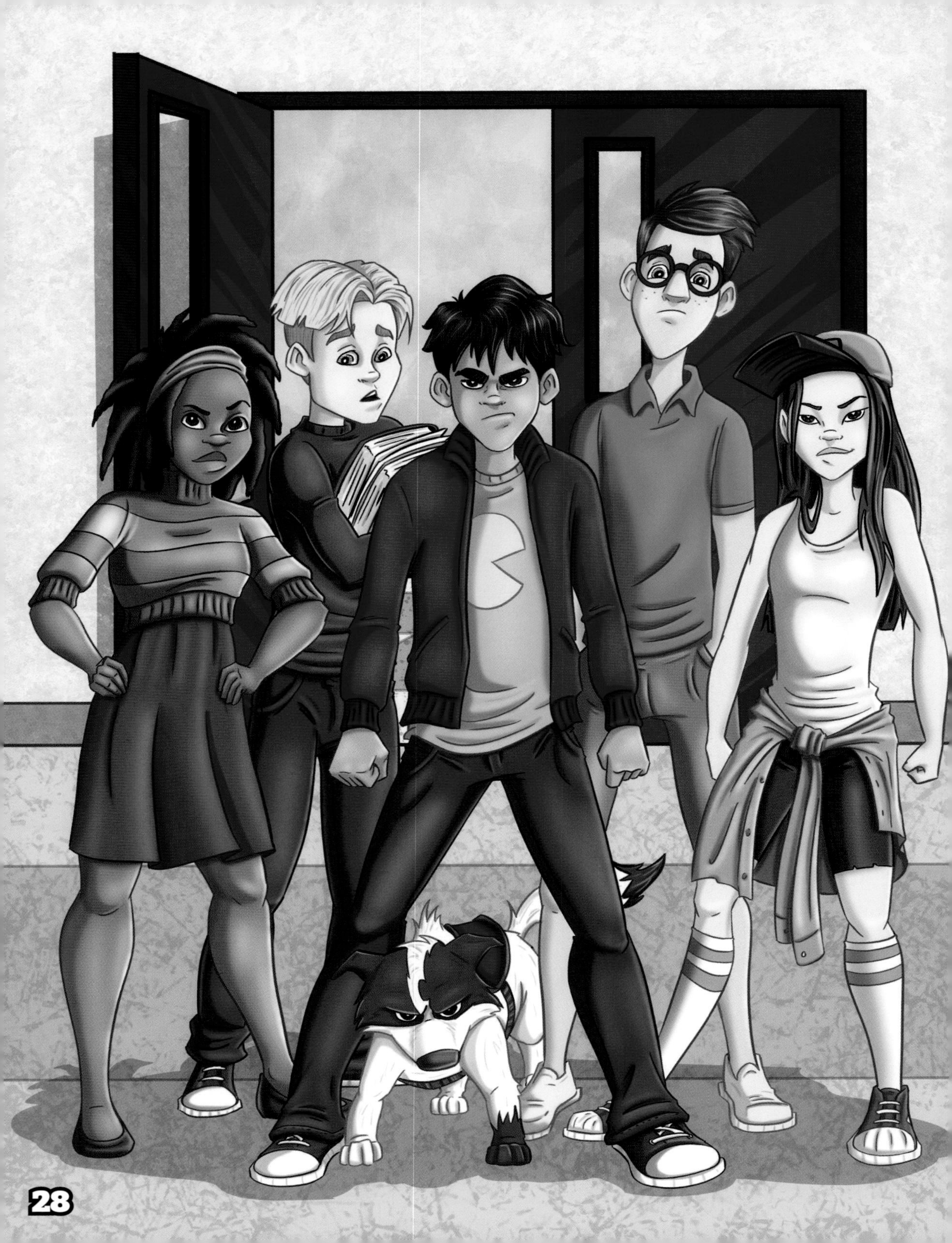

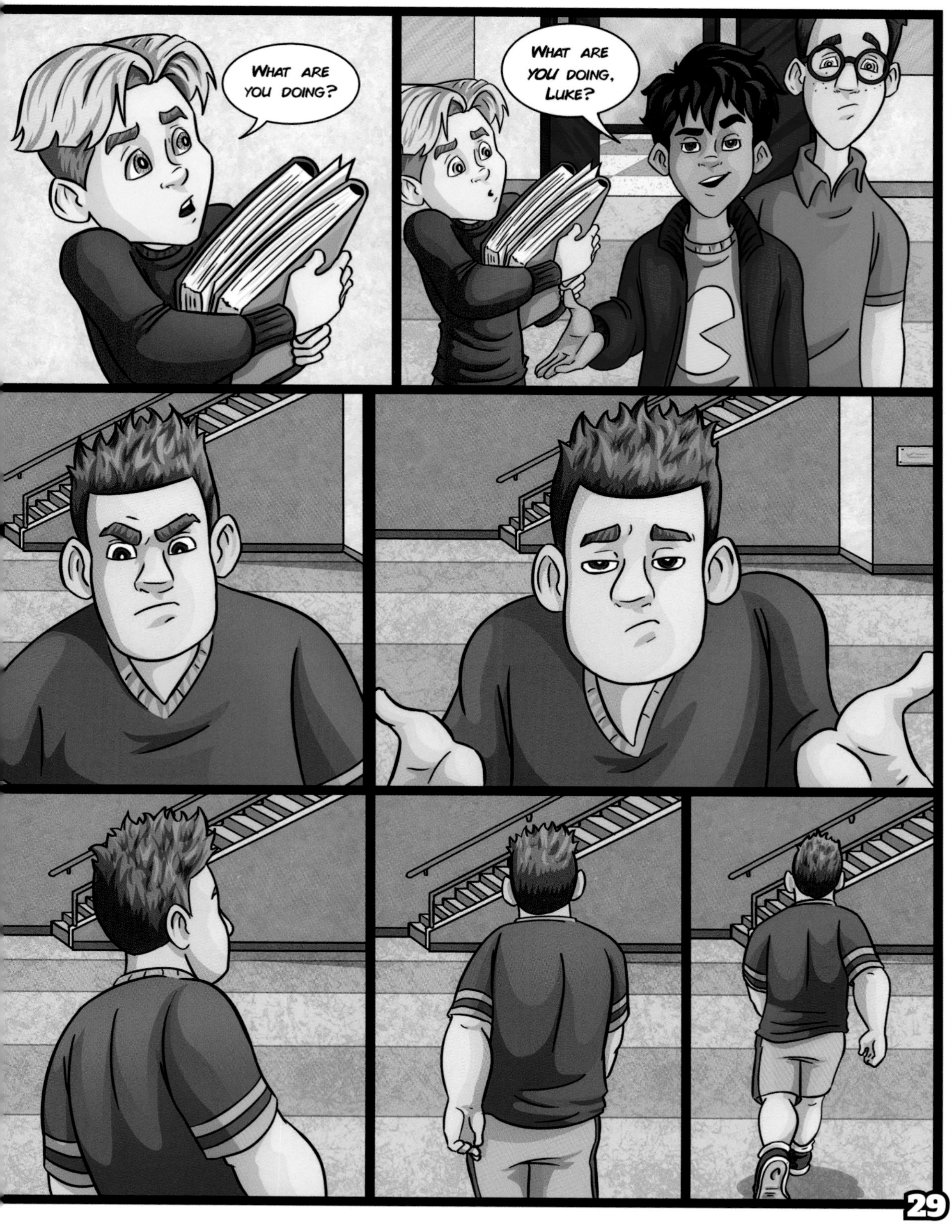
WHAT ARE YOU DOING?
WHAT ARE YOU DOING, LUKE?

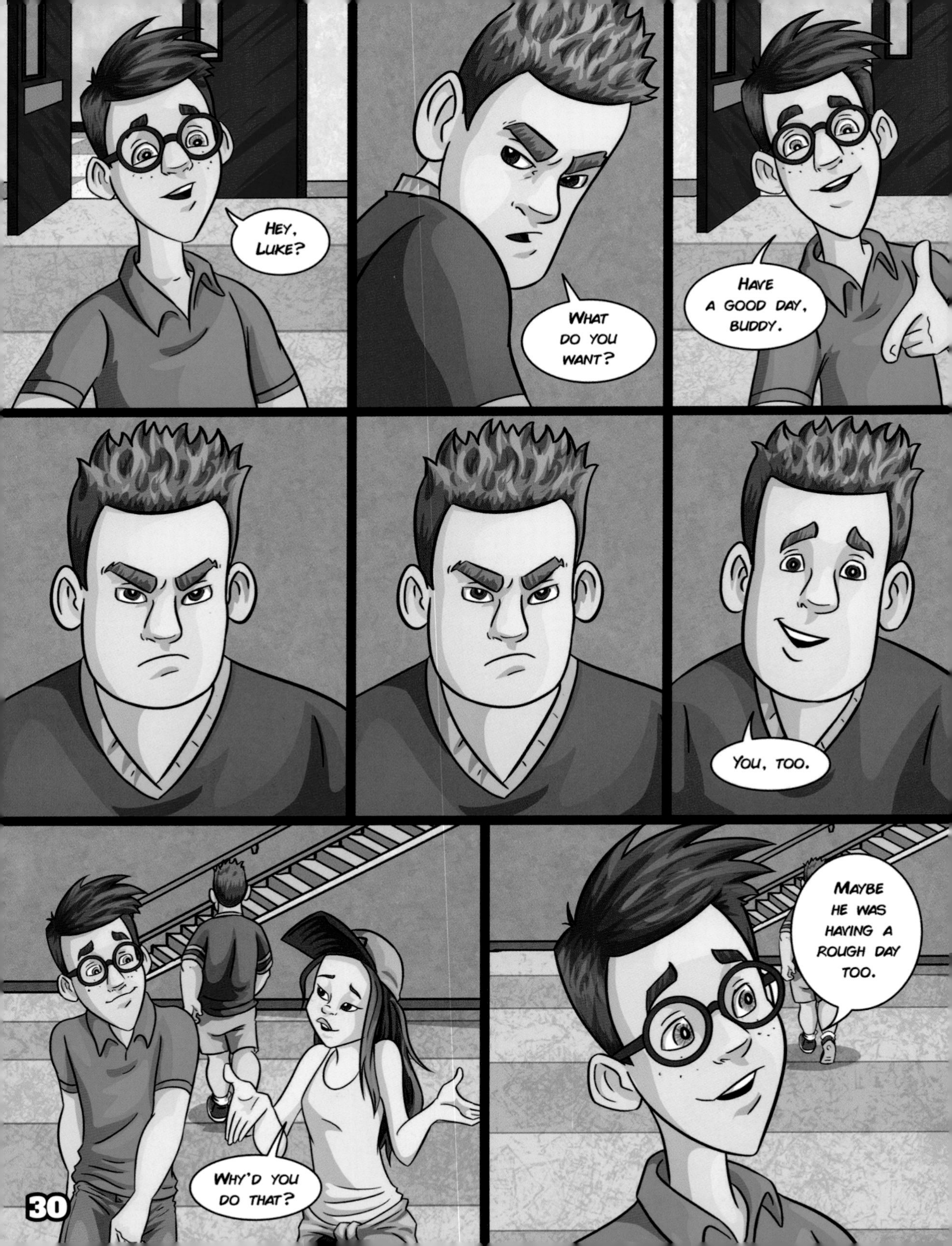
HEY, LUKE?
WHAT DO YOU WANT?
HAVE A GOOD DAY, BUDDY.
YOU, TOO.
WHY'D YOU DO THAT?
MAYBE HE WAS HAVING A ROUGH DAY TOO.

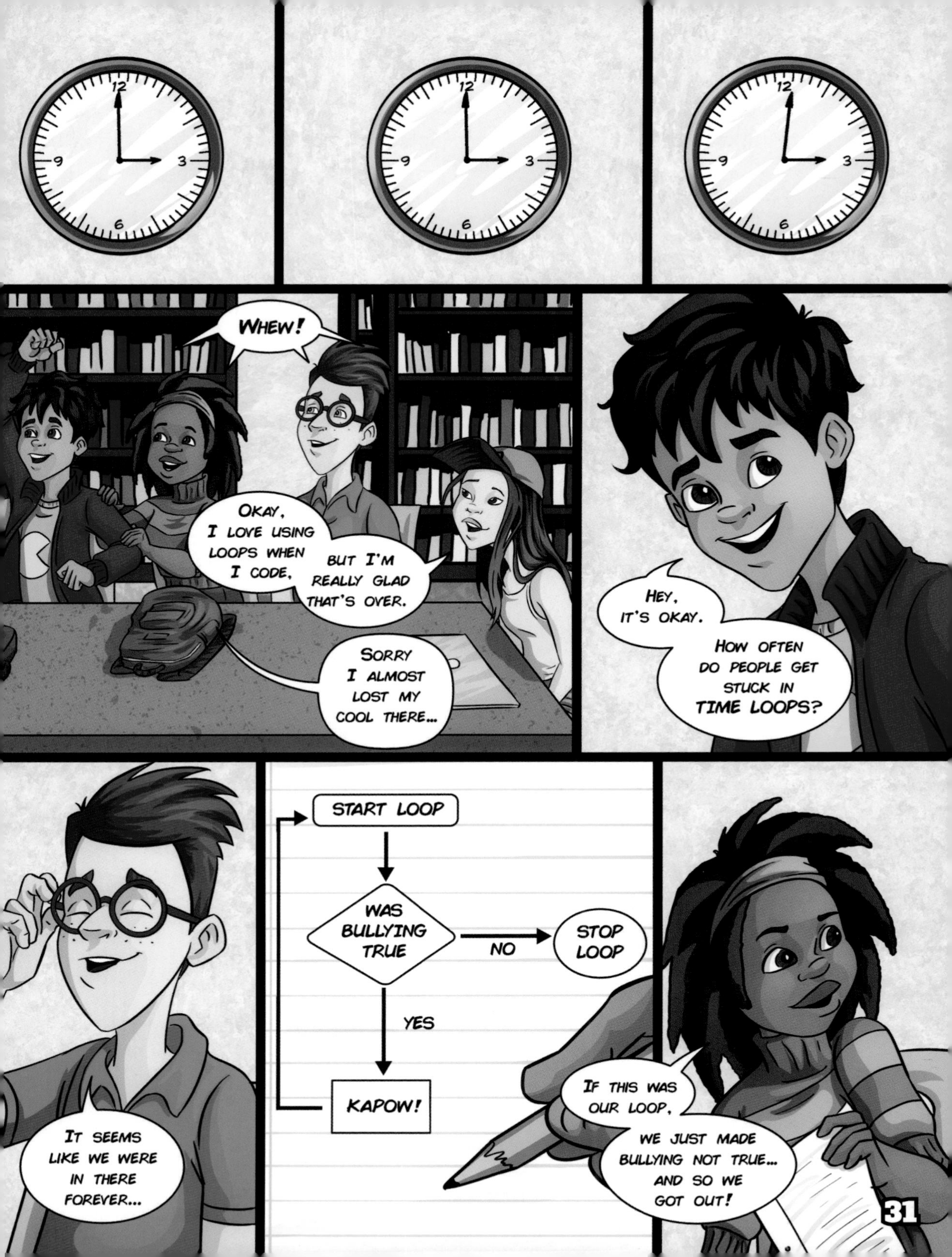

WHEW!
OKAY, I LOVE USING LOOPS WHEN I CODE,
BUT I'M REALLY GLAD THAT'S OVER.
SORRY I ALMOST LOST MY COOL THERE...
HEY, IT'S OKAY.
HOW OFTEN DO PEOPLE GET STUCK IN TIME LOOPS?
IT SEEMS LIKE WE WERE IN THERE FOREVER...
START LOOP
WAS BULLYING TRUE
NO
STOP LOOP
YES
KAPOW!
IF THIS WAS OUR LOOP,
WE JUST MADE BULLYING NOT TRUE... AND SO WE GOT OUT!

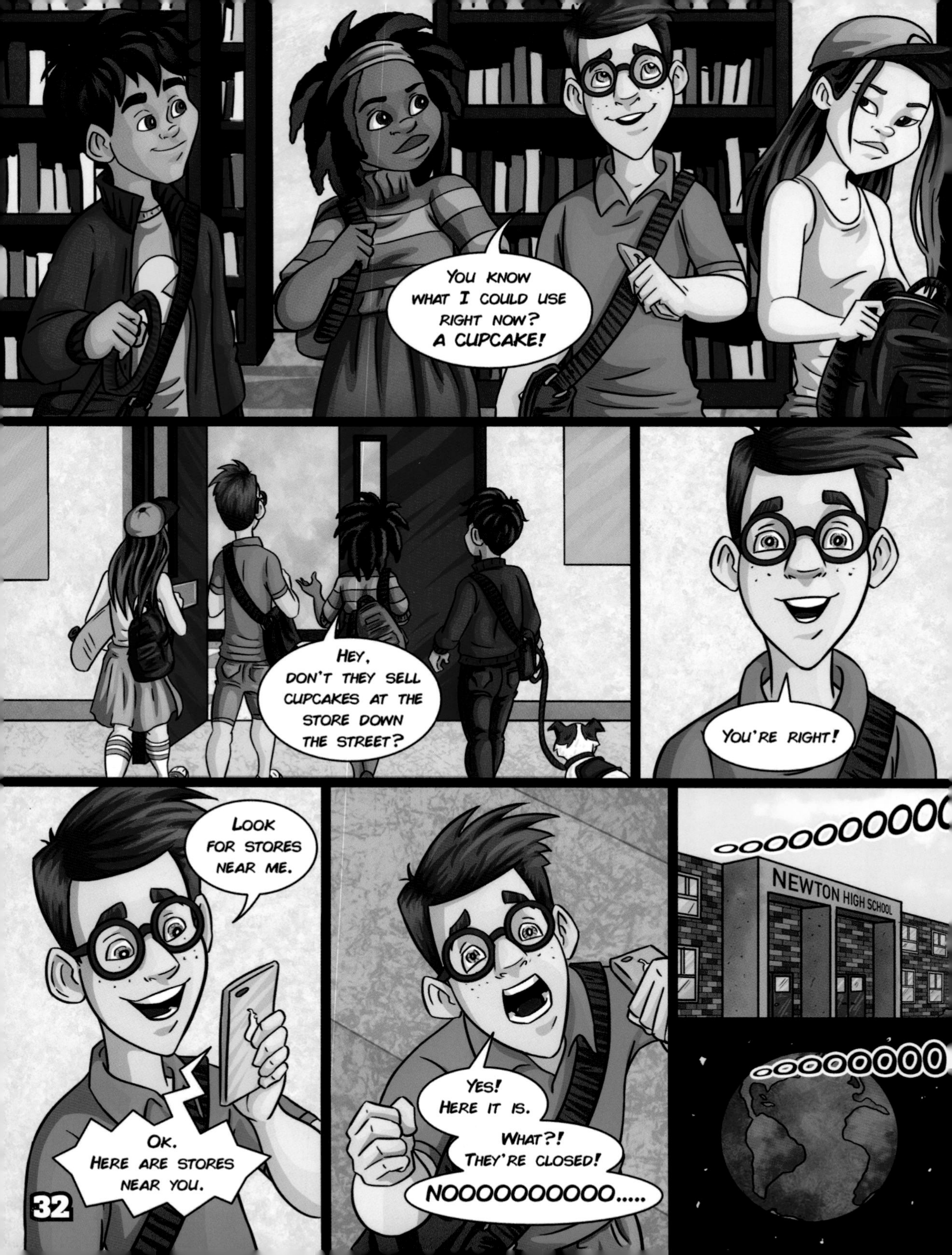
YOU KNOW WHAT I COULD USE RIGHT NOW? A CUPCAKE!
HEY, DON'T THEY SELL CUPCAKES AT THE STORE DOWN THE STREET?
YOU'RE RIGHT!
LOOK FOR STORES NEAR ME.
OK. HERE ARE STORES NEAR YOU.
YES! HERE IT IS.
WHAT?! THEY'RE CLOSED!
NOOOOOOOOOO.....
NEWTON HIGH SCHOOL
OOOOOOOOOOO
OOOOOOOOO